The SHINING LIGHT

The SHINING LIGHT

RUTH GLOVER

Beacon Hill Press of Kansas City
Kansas City, Missouri

ISBN: 083-411-514X

Printed in the
United States of America

Cover Design and Illustration: Keith Alexander

All Scripture quotations are from the King James Version of the Bible.

10   9   8   7   6   5   4

For my husband, Hal,
who always believed
I could do it

ABOUT THE AUTHOR

Ruth Vogt Glover was born and raised in Canada's central Saskatchewan bush country, of which she writes in this inspirational frontier romance novel, *The Shining Light*.

"The book is placed in the small farms of Donnybrook, the school district where I was born—near Macdowall and Prince Albert," she explains. "It was a hard life for adults, but for me as a child it was close to bliss. It is a wonderful place."

The author moved to Vancouver, Wash., in her late teens. It was in Vancouver she met Hal Glover, who finished his term in the Army and married Ruth in 1940. The couple attended Pasadena College (now Point Loma Nazarene College) together, where Rev. Glover earned a master of arts degree. He has pastored churches in California and the northwestern United States for many years, while Mrs. Glover has pursued her love of Christian writing.

That love has resulted in contributions to over 50 Christian publications, including the *Christian Standard*, *Decision*, the *Herald of Holiness*, *Home Life*, *Light and Life*, the *National Christian Reporter*, *Standard*, the *Sunday Digest*, *Vital Christianity*, *War Cry*, and the *Wesleyan Advocate*.

Mrs. Glover has returned numerous times to her native Saskatchewan to enjoy the land and to visit relatives. She and her husband now live in The Dalles, Oreg., the western terminus of the Oregon Trail. Rev. Glover pastors a church in the community while his wife gives support and continues her writing. They have three children and seven grandchildren.

The Shining Light is Mrs. Glover's first novel.

THE
SHINING
LIGHT

*H*e-e-e-ere, *chick chick chick!"*
     With the sky stretching endlessly blue over-
head, Abbie Rooney's feet were planted in the muck of a
poultry pen. With the fragrance of all outdoors just a
breeze away—a combination of late-blooming flowers,
ripening grain, freshly mowed meadow, and sun-dried
berries—Abbie's delicate nostrils flared with the odor of
damp feathers. And though field and sky resounded with
birdsong, her ears were filled with the clucks and cackles
of chickens bearing down on her from all directions. It was
enough to make one laugh—or cry.

     Abbie recognized the paradox of life in the bush, or
parkland, as some more euphemistically called it. She
called it "the bush," and it stretched across Saskatchewan
like a broad, green belt, dividing the prairies to the south
and the forests to the north. Verdant and lovely, it was land
to be prized—or shunned.

     Oh yes, it was beautiful. But it was also harsh. Even as
it promised, it threatened. As it gave, it took. The very
beauty of it, tangled brush and tall trees, shut house from
house and neighbor from neighbor.

     And yes, it could be bountiful; its black soil was capa-
ble of high yields. But a frost-free period of little more than

100 days made productivity uncertain. Fields, wondrously fertile, were pocked by countless gopher holes. Grain, though of good, hard quality, was decimated by unbelievable hordes of scavenging mice.

"Ya can't win for losin'!" old Hubert Runyon had declared when mosquitoes drove his horse, desperate for relief, into a slough, with Hubert and the plow right behind. Even the cooling dip for man and beast was spoiled by the menace of blood-sucking leeches lurking in the water.

Sunsets, as glorious as any in the world, were shattered more times than not by a loon's eerie cry, calling the soaring soul earthward. And a chicken's squawk could drown out the sweeter sound of one's own child! Abbie sighed as an insistent call from the house finally caught her attention.

"Ma-maaaaaa," Corcoran was shrilling. Or was it Cameron?

Abbie squinted into the glory of the morning. The child, aware that he had her attention at last, mouthed something, but it was lost in the hubbub as chickens, ducks, and a few graceless turkeys jostled each other raucously, their beaks stretching toward the pail in her hand.

Caught between the chickens at her feet and her "chicks"—Corcoran, Cameron, and Merry—in the house, all clamoring for their breakfast, Abbie threw a shining arc of grain around her and called, "I'll be in soon."

Shouted scraps of sentences from her son were lost in the nearer racket. Worth, Abbie's husband, appeared at the barn door and called an interpretation. "He wants to know if he can dish up the porridge."

"Absolutely not! *Corky! Stay away from the stove!*" Worth and Abbie were never quite free of concern for their children's health and well-being; the specter of illness, injury, and the long distance from medical aid was always with them.

But still she bawled the command. Abbie cringed to hear herself. "Mark it up as one more minus for the bush," she muttered.

But what, after all, did it matter? Who aside from Worth—and he was laughing at her—could hear? She might, she supposed sourly, run half-dressed across the yard, her hair on fire, shrieking to high heaven—and no one, no one in the whole wide world, would hear or see.

It wasn't that neighbors weren't reasonably near— homesteads were usually a quarter-section in size. It wasn't that they weren't caring—pioneers were bonded with a strong brotherhood. It was, simply, that the bush separated them into their own world as surely as though they were in solitary confinement. "A luxuriant prison," Abbie acknowledged, "but a prison nevertheless."

Abbie went back to feeding the chickens, wishing she hadn't been goaded into behavior she considered unbecoming to a lady. "But honestly," she fumed, "even a saint would be tested beyond endurance here!" Implied was the thought that, even in this, the bush was to blame.

Breakfast—oatmeal simmering on the back of the range—was ready, water was at a low boil for tea, and toast would brown quickly on the wide range top. When Worth finished milking Cinderella, named by the boys (they were big on fairy tales at the time), and had turned the cow into the pound with her bawling calf, Abbie would be ready to go into the house and begin Sunday's routine.

In the meantime she dawdled, enjoying the sun's early warmth on arms that had tanned and a nose that had freckled despite faithful consumption of Dr. Rose's Complexion Wafers. "Taken as directed," had been the guarantee that lured her into buying a dozen boxes, "the wafers will be found a positive, safe, and magical specific for all sorts of skin problems, unsightliness, and imperfections, a sure cure for freckles, blackheads, pimples, vulgar redness, rough, yellow, or muddy skin." Abbie touched her freckling nose and rued the lavishness and foolishness of her spending spree when she had made preparations for their move to the homestead in the bush.

A Rhode Island Red, pecking hopefully at the metal buckle on her boot, called Abbie back to reality. If she was to feed chickens and family, dress herself and the children, and be ready for the lengthy drive to the schoolhouse for Sunday service, she'd need to finish up and get indoors.

Dipping her slim, work-roughened hand into the battered pail, Abbie flung another handful of grain and couldn't resist a spontaneous laugh as the birds—legs churning, wings lifted, eyes glittering, and beaks agape— dashed for their food. It was such a ridiculous sight—and the morning was so beautiful, and the children were so precious, and Worth such a dear, and they would soon be meeting with new friends, to worship, and God was so good—that Abbie just had to laugh aloud.

The joyous sound spilled across the dew-drenched yard until it seemed to rebound from the green walls that circled her world. Abbie sobered; she and the bush had not come to terms.

Her gaze lifted to the three slim openings that broke the leafy enclosure: trails to the road, the garden, and the fields—tenuous threads of freedom. She watched as a crow, cawing stridently, lifted from a treetop to flap its way across the clearing toward the garden and the tender corn. "Consider the ravens," she muttered, "which neither have storehouse nor barn; and God feedeth them."

"That's all well and good for ravens," she sniffed. "As for chickens—it's up to me!"

But her eyes, as golden in their way as the grain she scattered (Worth's gallant comparison), softened at the sound of whistling from the low barn. Worth was invariably cheerful, full of confidence, undeniably a happy man. In the face of his contentment, his "dream come true," Abbie felt she could do no less than smile, however doggedly, speak encouragingly, and work willingly.

And I really don't mind the work, she told herself truthfully, even as she studied a broken fingernail and wondered how she would ever make her hands presentable for church. Nor the cramped living conditions in the little house. Nor the lack of emporiums or soda fountains or libraries or sidewalks. Even the separation from her family she could bear with fortitude, for Worth's sake.

Honesty prevailed again, and Abbie admitted that, all things considered, she and Worth were fortunate. "Blessed" would be a better word. "So far, so good" was her cautious assessment of their few months in the district of Wildrose. (Her favorite flower was the rose. But here in the Territories—wild, of course!) In spite of her fears, no medical emergency had arisen, no child had wandered away in the bush. The crop looked fair, and the animals were healthy. The Rooneys had survived a hectic spring and were weathering an exhausting summer. Winter—Abbie's thoughts skittered away from a northern winter. At least they would be well shod! And Abbie chuckled and groaned, with the same mix of delight and dismay that had marked her day thus far.

As overstocked on footwear as complexion wafers, Abbie had shamelessly plundered the family store before they sold it. She wondered, guiltily at times, if Worth had indulged her in her feverish buying spree, suspecting she was not all that thrilled about giving up her comfortable life for a lifetime on the frontier. Back home in Ontario, Worth had worked in his father's "Bootery and Leather Goods" store, and for the first 10 years of their marriage the young Rooneys had enjoyed the "good life." When Worth's father died, and his mother soon after, the business and other assets had been Worth's as the only surviving child. He hadn't hesitated: Sell! Move west! Homestead!

The speed with which her husband accomplished his goal left Abbie reeling. Obviously this was something Worth had dreamed about and planned for, with certain contacts made and costs figured. It was estimated, they were told, that a minimum of $1,000 was essential as capital for equipment, animals, and supplies to keep a family going until a crop could be harvested. Without cash, a settler was forced to find work wherever he could—trapping or fishing in the north or hiring on the railroad, sawmill or gristmill. Whatever the choice, it separated the family and put an almost unbearable burden on the wife and mother.

Thanks to Worth's inheritance, the Rooneys had arrived better fixed financially than many homesteaders; it would be Abbie's first item of praise at church this morning. But, of course, they weren't really homesteaders, having purchased their place outright from the speculator who had filed on it and who had cleared some land, built a log house and several outbuildings, and planted a crop.

Yes, Abbie reflected, she and Worth were blessed. They weren't separated, were well equipped, and had sufficient cash to see them through until the crop was in. Abbie breathed a sign of relief. Her spending before they ever arrived had been foolish, even laughable, but with good management from here on they would be fine.

Certainly they *looked* prosperous, she thought, as she glanced around—especially when compared to some of their neighbors, who looked desperately poverty-stricken, struggling to keep body and soul together. The adjoining homestead was a prime example; Abbie's thoughts shifted to the Jamesons. Theirs was a sad story.

What little Abbie knew of the Jamesons she had learned from Samuel Morris. The Morrises and Jamesons were her closest neighbors, one to the north, the other to the south of the farm that would henceforth be called "the Rooney place."

* * *

Sam had been Worth's contact and, as prearranged, was at the Meridian depot to greet the little family when the train pulled in. He had welcomed them warmly, his strong English accent standing out among the various Slavic, Scottish, and French accents that were vocal reminders of the disparate roots of these land seekers. Sam's kind heart and "good manners," as Abbie interpreted it, were apparent from the start. In him they would have a friend, and Abbie's tensions and anxieties eased somewhat.

Sam, Worth, and several helpful bystanders loaded the Rooneys' trunks and boxes into the wagon. The children ran with abandon around the obviously new station, finally free of the discomforts of the railroad car; Worth paused long enough to dig out a few coppers, and they went happily to the settlement's one general store for peppermints. After some thought, Abbie followed to lay in a supply of food, anticipating their arrival at the raw homestead with its unfurnished cabin (except for the kitchen range, which the previous owner had agreed to leave) and the urgency of a meal as soon as they got there.

"We'll come back tomorrow and get your household goods," Sam promised. "I guess you can bunk around tonight . . . ?" Worth, after an uneasy glance at his wife, assured him they would manage.

Ready to go at last, the children, cheeks bulging and fingers sticky, were hoisted into the wagon and to seats on packing boxes. Worth stood behind the spring seat, where Abbie, after she was assisted by Sam, took her place with a tired Merry on her lap.

Sam, middle-aged, gnarled like a wind-tortured tree but strengthened through the ordeal, climbed up beside Abbie after tucking away a few packages and the mail about which he said, "Regina, my wife, looks for these letters from home—from England, I should say. *This* is home now."

And it's to be our home, Abbie realized with some surprise; the finality of their decision was only beginning to seep past the trials and trauma of a move of thousands of miles, dozens of good-byes, and buckets of farewell tears.

Almost immediately the small hamlet disappeared from view, lost in a leafy embrace as they wended their way over the tracks, across the road toward Wildrose. The area was well named. "But so are some of the other districts," Sam said. "There's Deer Run, for instance, Duck Lake, Moose Jaw."

Sam, of course, being one of the early settlers, had been over the road often. And being a friendly person, he seemed to know everyone along the route.

"First of all," he explained, "you'll notice that the better developed places are those nearest the railroad. That land was taken first. Latecomers, like you folks, have to go further back. We chose Wildrose even though other possibilities were available to us when we came. Never been sorry. Some folks," he said, slanting a speculative look at Abbie, "love the bush. Others are, well, intimidated by it."

"It's yielding, though, to hard work," Worth commented as they passed a small clearing where a sweat-soaked man paused in his grubbing to lean on his grub hoe, wipe his brow, and wave.

"Indeed. But given a chance, it springs back." Sam waved. "That man and his family," he explained, "came by Red River cart, lumbering along with precious few possessions."

The Saskatchewan River, Sam explained, had at one time been the highway of the fur traders; later, steamboats plied the fickle waterway and settlers came by both portage and boat. By the middle of the century the Red River cart had become the general all-purpose transport vehicle, being light yet strong, able to carry a ton of weight. "With wheels removed, it floats like a raft," Sam said.

The rattling wagon suddenly seemed like a grand conveyance indeed to Abbie, and she resolved to count her blessings.

"Now here," Sam said, rounding a curve and nodding toward a low cabin almost entirely surrounded by bush and trees, "are people almost as newly arrived as you folks." Smoke lifted from a tin stovepipe, the door stood open (Abbie shuddered to think of the flies the housewife had to contend with), and a few chickens scrabbled in the yard. Under the trees a woman struggled over a tub set on a trestle, and a clothesline sagged with the weight of water-soaked, heavy garments, mute evidence of her wearying task. But she straightened her back and waved cheerily.

"Whoa!" Sam pulled the team to a halt, reached below his feet, and pulled up a wrinkled envelope. Lifting it above his head, he waved it, and at a gesture from the woman, a towheaded boy sped down the lane toward the waiting wagon. Puffing, he reached a brown hand for the letter, blue eyes twinkling in a sunburned face.

"T'anks," he grinned, his eyes fixed on the twins, who suddenly turned shy, squirming on the box and reddening under the strange boy's scrutiny.

"Miko—," Sam began.

"Mike," the boy said.

"Mike," Sam smiled, "these are the Rooneys. You'll get to know them one of these days. Ask your folks if you can ride over and play sometime. OK?"

"OK," Mike said, and his grin, though mischievous, was warm. Manfully, he spat into the dirt at his feet, then turned on quick bare feet to take the mail to his mother.

"Hungarians," Sam said. "Besides being poor, they've got the extra problem of not knowing the language. I've been in their house—furniture made of boards and boxes."

"They're to be admired," Abbie said, with her first uneasy pang about the abundance of things they had brought with them, things she was beginning to believe might be useless (even ridiculous?) in the face of the stark needs of people like these.

"These buildings all seem substantial," Worth commented. "At least people don't have to live in the soddies we noted across the prairies."

Sam agreed. "That's one thing we have lots of—trees. Men get together for a house-raising and get a cabin up in a hurry. The smaller they are, the easier to heat, of course. Your cabin, as I mentioned in our correspondence, has four small rooms, with a kitchen added on. Not bad for a beginning. And starting off with your place set up, that's a help."

"It is," Abbie acknowledged humbly, taking another look at the cabin surrounded by fresh-cut stumps. But at the window a brave scrap of bright curtain waved, and the clearing was adrift with pink fireweed. Not realizing it was to set a pattern in her thinking, Abbie recognized for the first time the rawness of life in the bush, and the beauty. These people, it was clear, were here to stay. The buildings, though crude, were solid. They would make a go of it, if it meant bleaching their bones along the way. Some, sadly, had already paid the ultimate price. Many more would.

"Now here is the Jameson place," Sam said, breaking into Abbie's thoughts as she swayed almost hypnotically on the spring seat, fighting the temptation to fall asleep (and fall off!).

Sam nodded in the direction of a gaunt frame house coming into view beyond a particularly thick stand of trees. "And this is the beginning of the district of Wildrose."

Sam turned briefly to look over his shoulder at the twins, who had climbed off the box to stare after the disappearing boy, Mike. "From here on," he explained, "the young'uns attend the Wildrose school." With a glance at Merry, he added, "Don't know about the little girl."

"Merry is only three," Abbie murmured, hitching the weary child higher on her lap.

"The Jamesons don't have any children—now," Sam said briefly.

Abbie studied the cluster of buildings. The contrast to the last farm was striking. The unpainted house had weathered to a dull gray; the outbuildings were equally drab—a charcoal drawing in an exquisite frame. Except that a dog set up a perfunctory barking, the sound issuing from the silent scene in an aloof, disembodied way, one might have imagined the place was derelict, abandoned. Abbie gave an involuntary shiver, the first of many, she was to realize later.

"Dreary," Sam said with a sigh. "But it wasn't always that way. Once there was laughter, and romping . . .

"No one cares how it looks now, leastwise not Dora. And Jamie doesn't have the time, and probably not the heart, for it. Flowers and things like that depend on the woman, right?"

Sam slanted another look at Abbie, and it seemed to her his glance took in her hands, white and soft, as they clasped Merry to her, and her slim feet (beautifully shod!) propped on the front of the wagon beside his battered boots.

"Women don't have it easy here," Sam said.

"The Jamesons," Abbie said quickly. "You said they have no children—now?"

"Dorrie and Jamie lost their two boys about three years ago. Diphtheria."

The first feeling of compassion for the couple welled up in Abbie's heart.

"How sad," she breathed, tightening her hold on the drowsy Merry, and craning to embrace the twins in a soft look.

Worth, at Abbie's back, slipped his arms around his wife's waist and drew her against him, silently reminding her of his presence and strength.

With a cluck to the horses and a flap of the reins on their broad backs, Sam hurried the wagon past the Jameson place.

"You'll meet them at church, most likely. That is, if you folks are in the habit of going."

"We go," Abbie said, a little stiffly. "Usually."

"You'll go here," Sam said wisely. "You'll go if you get lonely enough, and most folks do."

What an idea! Attending church because you are lonely. What a reason for worship!

As though he sensed Abbie's reaction, Sam said gently, "For an isolated homesteader, meeting time is salvation, in more ways than one. In the winter, when travel is worst, we have the best attendance."

Abbie looked puzzled.

"Housebound, tired of looking at four walls, hungry to hear someone else's voice—even the preacher's," and Sam grinned.

While Abbie thought about that, Sam returned to the Jamesons: "Trouble is, they don't go very often."

Abbie, lost in thought, looked at him blankly.

"The Jamesons—Dora and Jamie," Sam explained. He hesitated, adding with what may have been a certain delicacy, "Dora has never been quite . . . right since they lost the boys."

The story hinted at was a chilling one, and Abbie gave her second shiver. Worth's arms tightened.

Two boys, and both dead! Abbie twisted in Worth's embrace, as though to reassure herself of her sons' sturdy presence. Corcoran and Cameron were hanging over the tailgate, spitting into the dust of the road.

"You watch!" Abbie's mother had foretold darkly, and it seemed Abbie could hear her now. Crying out against the situation that would take her loved ones far from her, the anguished grandmother had warned, "Those boys will turn into wild Indians!"

But the Indians weren't wild. As for the métis, those proud people of mixed blood, following their uprising and the bitter Riel Rebellion, they had joined their full-blooded brothers on the reserves or, under the North-West Half-Breed Commission, applied for land scrip. They were now accepted by fellow farmers with comparatively little ill will.

Wild Indians was one concern Abbie didn't have. The boys, if anything, were in danger of turning into spitting hooligans! Right now Abbie was too tired to tackle the problem.

But when the lonely Jameson homestead and its desolate buildings had disappeared, enveloped in bush until even the dog's bark was smothered into silence, Abbie knew what it was she feared: the bush.

* * *

With the autumn sun warming her body, a perennial chill held Abbie's heart in a grip that had not loosed its hold since the day of introduction to the bush, and which, at times, threatened to overwhelm her. The move—it seemed so final. This life, hers by decree rather than choice, was it to be *forever?* The permanency of their setup suggested it, Worth's happy whistle attested to it, the children's pure joy confirmed it. She alone yearned for escape and, loving Worth, knew it was out of the question.

Lifting her face to the sky, ignoring the cacophony at her feet, Abbie prayed the most unselfish prayer of her young life: *O Father! If this is where You want me, help me accept it! If this is the path of Your choosing, teach me to walk it willingly, even*—it was hard to finish—*even happily.*

*T*he morning dew sparkled no brighter than the tears that trembled on Abbie's lashes when Worth's whistle, which had been muted by the sturdiness of the log barn, erupted with the chorus of "Dairy Maid Waltz" when he stepped through the barn door, milk pail in hand.

Abbie could often locate Worth by his whistling. Usually she could tell what he was doing. On the way to the fields it was apt to be "Meadows O' Green." Chopping wood or filling the wood box it was "The Hearth Is the Heart of the Home." At dawn it was "O Gold Sun, upon Arising," to dusk's "In the Gloaming," with a dozen others in between.

Worth straightened his slim figure and turned in Abbie's direction. The whistle died on his lips (had he seen the tears glinting on her cheeks?), and his eyes seemed to cling to hers. Even at this distance she could see the question clouding their gray depths.

The truth burst upon Abbie, and she wondered why she hadn't known it before: *He knows!* Perhaps it was an instant's vulnerable expression on his face that betrayed him.

Softly he began to whistle "Don't Be Angry with Me, Darling," and there was no doubt. Worth knew. Worth knew her fears and her discontent. But he didn't know about her prayer.

Dashing the tears from her cheeks, Abbie tipped the pail upside down, tossed the remaining chicken feed to the ground, and turned with decisive steps to join her husband. Her smile was warm, and it was real. With Romeo and Juliet dangerously underfoot (Worth also read Shakespeare to the boys), tails aloft, meowing piteously for milk, Worth strode toward Abbie, his face once again reflecting the good humor with which he faced life.

But a grin flickered across his lips as he watched Abbie step from the chicken yard and latch the gate carefully behind her; they had had their differences where the fowl were concerned. Not for Abbie a yard with chickens running free!—hers would be neatly penned, thank you! It was not, mind you, because coyotes or other four-legged marauders might make off with the poultry but because she couldn't endure the thought of her children's bare feet squishing through a chicken-messed yard.

As for the bare feet—Worth had won that round. "They'll run free in the summer like other farm youngsters," he said firmly. And who could blame them for wanting to shed heavy boots when at last the earth warmed and the rich soil begged to be handled and felt, by hand and foot, by plow and harrow?—even when those boots were the finest that Rooney's Bootery had to offer!

"Look out, cat!" Abbie came close to stumbling over Romeo. "For heaven's sake. Is the whole world hungry?"

"Count me in," Worth said affably and led the way to the house.

Clumping along at his side, shod in her matching "Heavy Buckle Arctics," Abbie couldn't resist a glance at the shed and a thought for the beautiful leatherbound trunk and handsome fitted Gladstone bags, numerous boxes and crates, stuffed with items they hadn't been able to fit into the cramped house—worse yet, items that had no need to fit into the house. Every day that passed made some of them seem more useless.

Buying and packing had been fun, making a game of what Abbie had dared not think of as being deadly serious. And if buying and packing had been fun, *un*packing and sorting, when they reached Wildrose, had its funny moments, although they seemed at times more hysterical than humorous.

"I bet we're the only family in the entire Northwest to have a patent shoe stretcher," Worth had joked, adding, "What we really need is a shoehorn."

"But we have several," Abbie had begun, sifting through numerous kinds of laces, heel lifts, shoe plates, shoe buttons, and heel-and-toe circlets.

"I mean one big enough to get everything into the cabin! Now these, Madam," Worth intoned, picking up several sets of "Non-Crumpling Insoles" and dangling them between thumb and forefinger, "are made of gen-u-wine horsehair, with a fine steel stay running the full length. They come with a guarantee to lay flat, without ruffling or crumpling!"

"Well, who needs a ruffled insole?" Abbie giggled. "But oh, Worth," she wailed, "what about *these* ruffles?" She dipped into a box of fine nainsook and high-quality cambric dresses. Embroidered ruffles, fancy braid, extravagant tucks, and lace edging made each small dress eminently unsuitable for frontier life. "Merry will outgrow them before she can possibly use them. And that's if they're practical, which they're not!"

"Keep out two or three," Worth said sensibly. "After all, we go to church—usually." He grinned as he reminded Abbie of her response to Sam's inquiry about their church-going habits.

Abbie threw a beaded chatelaine purse at him and then rescued it, wrapped it tenderly in a length of cardinal-colored jacquard silk, and folded it away. Their fun and games raveled rather quickly to dismay as their useless purchases mounted: carpet stretcher (and their linoleum was fortunate to have a few small rugs scattered over it); "modern" lemon squeezer ("Abbie, where do you think you're going—Florida?"); "never-root" hog tamer (and their pig, Porcelina, was concerned only with sleeping and eating); and a straw helmet that Worth, with some violence, refused to so much as set on his head.

"Do you suppose we could sell some of these things?" Abbie asked dubiously, and Worth hooted, "Dreamer! Unless we can demonstrate that a lemon squeezer will crack wild hazelnuts or dehorn a calf, we're stuck with it!"

Each of these they had packed (hidden!) away, along with several sets of satin damask linen towels (white!) and enough mufflers, capes, shawls, and fascinators to clothe the entire Territory.

Aside from fishing out books and a few comforters, they had found no reason to open the shed except to stuff more useless items away. Perhaps it was because they had done a thorough job of sorting; more likely it was because—with their funds shrinking and their foolish spending becoming ever more obvious—they found little to be amused about and much to regret, and they didn't want to be reminded of either.

Approaching the house, where the children danced an impatient jig behind a screen door (no flies in the kitchen for Abbie!), with Worth carrying the pail of milk and the cats meowing at his heels, Abbie brightened. "Admit it, Worth," she twinkled. "I made at least one good purchase."

"A frying pan?" he suggested, with breakfast overdue and the clamors of three children and two cats in his ears.

"That too," she said.

And Worth and Abbie paused before entering their house, to scrape their matching "Heavy Buckle Arctics," made of vaunted "first-quality pure gum rubber and fine Jersey cloth fashioned on a handsome coin last," on a skateblade nailed upside down on the step. Not for Abbie a muck-tracked linoleum!

*H*arry Runyon stepped outside, holding the door knob momentarily until he was certain of his balance. Then with cautious steps he crossed the rough boards of the small porch, to teeter there until his hand grasped the upright that supported the overhang. With the other gnarled hand he fumbled at the odd button or two on his baggy sweater.

"Hey, Hu," he called over his shoulder. "Better put on your sweater. It's nippy out here."

The scene seemed to repeat itself. Another aged man creaked from the shadows of the house, balanced with care, and moved with equal caution toward the porch's other upright.

"Harry, you ninny," this second apparition scolded mildly, "it ain't winter."

"It ain't? Well, whatever season is it, Hu?"

"Wouldn't do no good to tell you, Harry. You'd forget before you got your sweater unbuttoned."

"Your forgetter's as good as mine, Hu. Don't forget *that!*"

Hubert Runyon snorted; it was a response he practiced numerous times a day in conversation with his brother.

"You really ought to do something about that problem, Hu," Harry said now, as he often did. "Ever think of a handkerchief?"

"I think, all right," Hu responded now, as he usually did. "But then I remember it's upstairs in the dresser drawer, and I think again. Anyway," he added, "that's not the problem. The problem is that you're so aggravatin', so stubborn, you're such a—a curmudgeon." Proper descriptions failing, and being out of breath anyway, Hubert subsided.

"I am, ain't I?" Harry agreed smugly. "But I'll tell you one thing I'm not." Harry waited.

"Spit it out, Harry!"

"Cold. I'm not cold, Hu, and you're shakin'. Or have you been standin' up too long?"

Hubert straightened his sagging knees, drew a large breath of the clear, crisp autumn air into his lungs, coughed, clung to the post, and finally managed, "Well, I'm not goin' back in now that I've got out here. Probably wouldn't make it out again for another three weeks."

The elderly brothers stood in companionable silence, their faded eyes studying the neglected farmyard, the empty pound, the vacant barn, the silent pens. Hubert's gaze swung, as it often did, to a second house, not far away, identical to the one at his back. But empty—so empty—but no emptier than Hubert's eyes.

"Seems like yesterday, Hu," Harry said gently, "when you was comin' out of that green door (Hubert had painted his door green; Harry's door was red, the only difference in the two-story log structures), only you was usually jumpin', runnin' before you hit the ground."

"Had to keep up with you, Harry," Hu said softly. "Always had to keep up with you."

"Well," Harry said bracingly, after a moment's reflection, "see if you can do it again—keep up with me, that is."

And with a sigh, the brothers turned from the memory of days too quickly over, too sweet to forget.

Harry reached behind him for a knobbed walking stick, whittled painfully from one of his own poplar trees when the "rheumatics" first struck. Hu, still keeping up with his brother, had carved his cane soon after, and he reached for it now.

With great care, much mumbling ("Why'd we make these steps so high, anyway?"), and considerable chaffing of each other, Harry and Hubert stepped down to the ground—two old men with unkempt beards and disreputable hats, wearing much-spotted, old-fashioned clothes and boots that had seen better days, better because muscles hadn't atrophied, lungs shrunk, eyes dimmed, hands stiffened; better because each day had brought a challenge to wrest their homestead from the reluctantly surrendering bush; better because behind a green door and a red door Bessie and Virgie hummed as they went about tasks that made the identical houses, erected by look-alike brothers, places of comfort and centers of contentment.

Now the green and red doors had faded until even they resembled each other. Now one house was closed; now two mounds of dirt settled earthward in the cemetery.

Now days dragged by in a blur where very little happened to distinguish one from another. Now stretching hours were spent in rocking chairs at the side of a wood heater and naps were routine, the endless stillness broken only by the occasional snore or the popping of the fire.

Now meals were highpoints—and horrors. Now laundry was piled in bedroom corners awaiting the arrival of a concerned neighbor—usually Carolyn Morris—who would give a day to a flurry of washing and ironing, with a little housecleaning thrown in.

Now the Monday, Wednesday, and Friday visits of Willie Tucker were as anticipated as though he were Santa

Claus, and the supplies he brought were as welcome as Christmas presents. Now a call from Pastor Victor assumed the importance of a visit from the Lord himself.

Now a walk outside was a big event.

"Now that we're here, Hu," Harry quavered as he and Hubert made their slow way across the yard, "can you recollect why?"

"Well, it wasn't to pick peas!" Hu said smartly as they passed a weedy, empty garden spot. "At least I s'pose not; we don't have no pails with us."

"You get sassier the longer you live, Hu," Harry clucked. "Plumb makes me dread old age."

Hubert attempted a snort, but the effort almost cost him his balance; Harry, fearing a similar result if he should indulge in a laugh at his brother's expense, contented himself with a grin.

But they knew where they were headed; the burgeoning grain had awakened feelings that had been muted, not quenched, by the years; every instinct in their frail bodies was to respond to autumn in the time-honored way: get the crop harvested.

Hubert and Harry had roused themselves to what was, for them, tingling activity. Changing felt slippers for boots, to which ancient shreds of manure had bonded, they had banked the fire, located shapeless headgear, and donned—in Harry's case—a worn sweater, and headed for the nearest wheat field.

In its way, it was a trip down memory lane. Passing the outhouse, the only edifice to which there remained any sign of a well-used path, they reached the garden plot where two calico-clad figures had once bent energetically to a satisfying task; silently they passed the graveyard of their rusty plow, mower, and reaper. Dulled ears could imagine the sounds of horses stamping heavy feet in the depths of the empty barn; nostrils quivered to the remembered scent of steamy manure, sweet hay, and warm milk streaming into a pail clutched between bent knees. A shaft of sunlight through the open door lit a spot on a stall where cows had, over long years through endless winter days, rubbed a hip until the wood shone like the handsomest sideboard in a king's palace.

And unsteady feet shuffled on, and minds, still sharp, remembered, and hearts overflowed.

*   *   *

Harry and Hubert didn't really know their origins; they weren't even sure of their ages. Even their name, Runyon, wasn't their real name. Rather, it was the sound two small boys made when, with a strange accent, they had tried to pronounce it to anyone who cared to ask. And those who cared were few and far between. Two more waifs on the city streets of New York were of little consequence among the hodgepodge of newcomers flocking the docks and flooding the tenements.

Somewhere in this maelstrom Harry and Hubert had found themselves alone; they were never to know what happened to their parents. Whether they had deliberately abandoned their children, become ill, died, or been taken advantage of by sharpsters was a mystery. Eventually a concerned minister had collected some of the city's ragged urchins, placing them in an orphanage. Here, for a few years, Harry and Hubert had been fed and housed and received the only schooling they were to have. But when the building burned to the ground and pandemonium resulted, the boys took to the streets again. They survived, finding work where they could and shelter in a tenement with other men and boys no better off than they.

Though their early days were obscure, they never doubted they were brothers. For one thing, their resemblance to each other was remarkable. More, they invariably saw eye to eye on everything. Eventually Harry was to say, in the bantering manner that, even then, marked their relationship, "You'll have to get your own girl, Hu. This'n is mine." And Hu did, picking a girl as nearly like his brother's as could be found—her sister.

But to find them they had to leave the slums. Bidding city life good-bye, and without regrets, they hopped a train and headed for the open spaces, eventually working on a farm in Iowa. Here they found Bessie and Virgie, and from here, full of vigor, eager for new experiences, and ready for a challenge, they left for the vast Northwest Territories.

The Dominion government, to encourage settlement of the Canadian west, offered free land in the form of 160-acre homesteads; it was an opportunity that two landless, homeless, hopeful young men found irresistible. Trainloads of homeseekers went to see the land in response to advertisements placed by Canada's minister of the interior in thousands of weekly and farm newspapers in the U.S. and millions of booklets, all telling of the advantages offered. Little towns sprang up overnight; soddies dotted the prairies flourishing with golden grain. In the bush, farther north, fields were grubbed painstakingly, and cabins went up.

When the railroads petered out, the young couples loaded their few possessions on ox carts and penetrated the bush until, in its green heart, they found the location of their dreams. Life was hard, but it was good. Game was abundant, neighbors few. As the one decreased, the other increased, until farms, by and large, provided the settlers with their food, and friend helped friend through good times and bad. Hubert and Harry had never regretted their choice regarding their location or their wives.

And, still alike, neither couple had produced children. Happy and content as they were, it hadn't mattered too much—until now, that is. Now the two widowers, aside from each other, had no one. Now they realized they were no longer self-reliant. Now they daily grew more dependent on those selfsame neighbors who had become "family" across the years but who, in fact, were not blood related. And for two independent men, it was a painful situation.

When Bessie and Virgie had died of pneumonia in the same winter, the two aging men had closed Hu's house and moved into Harry's, ending their days as they had begun them—together.

Willie Tucker was an answer to prayer.

Praying had always been left to Bessie and Virgie. But there came a day when, alone, with problems bigger than they could handle, Harry had turned to Hu: "Hu," he said with unusual seriousness, "somebody in this house needs to pray. Get busy. See if the good Lord has a solution for us. We have to find someone to work our fields."

"Hey," Hu objected, "you always was better'n me; leastwise you always said you was. The good Lord will hear you quicker'n He'll hear me."

It wasn't a subject to be argued about, and eventually both old men bowed their heads, clasped their hands, and voiced their need.

When Willie Tucker, their neighbor, came over with an offer to work their fields, plant their grain, harvest their crop, and do it on shares, Harry and Hubert looked at each other, faded eyes alight. "Willie," they said, as they shook hands on the deal, "did you ever know you were an answer to prayer?"

Of course Willie didn't know. Willie never knew how often he was an answer to prayer. In a time and place where neighborliness was a way of life, where people needed each other, often desperately, and backwoods communities were bonded together by mutual need, Willie Tucker stood out.

It was Willie they called when there was a death, right along with the minister; Willie, whether he liked it or not (no one ever thought to wonder) was chief undertaker. Willie, in spite of his own farm and full load of work, somehow took on chores when illness or injury laid up the man of the house. Willie served on the school board, although he had no children (he had never married; no one thought it was necessary, for he functioned very well alone); he was a respected deacon in the church and was a general handyman when one was needed. "Willie'll do it" was a familiar phrase in the households of Wildrose.

There was a giving quality about Willie, but it was done in a quiet, self-effacing way, and he was often taken advantage of. But Willie never complained. "After all," he reasoned, "they have their families, and I have no one."

Willie's farm had been homesteaded by his parents, his father died young, and Willie took over the farm's work and the care of his mother. When she passed away, Willie slipped naturally into bachelorhood and, as far as anyone knew, was satisfied.

But in a way typical of Willie, he had noted, and pondered, the Runyon men's predicament. And he had come up with a solution, an "answer to prayer."

"It will benefit me too," he had responded, setting aside their attempts to thank him with the diffidence they had all come to expect.

It had worked out well; for several years Willie had produced the Runyon crop. It had given the brothers a living.

But along the way, as Hubert's and Harry's small strength waned more and more, Willie took on added responsibilities. He did their buying, he chopped their wood, he drew their water. He took their last cow and their small flock of chickens to his place, and he brought fresh milk, butter, and eggs three times a week.

Far more than renter of the Runyon fields, Willie had become deliveryman, adviser, repairman, butcher, mailman, and many other things to the two elderly men. Indoors, for the most part, the brothers struggled on by themselves; eventually they were overwhelmed by piles of dirty clothes, sticky floors, unwashed quilts, and grimy windows. And heaven alone knew how they survived on their own cooking.

It was no wonder they regarded Carolyn Morris as a "ministering angel" and another answer to their prayers. Carolyn had been a favorite in the childless Runyon households since her birth, when Virgie and Bessie had gone to the Morris homestead to help. Across the years they had delighted in being aunties to this lonely little girl whose relatives were far away in England.

When "Caro" fell from a tree when she and her brother Collum were hunting crows' nests, suffering a severe injury, the bonds had grown even closer. With her physical activities curtailed drastically, Carolyn had become withdrawn, quiet, wan; a visit to the Runyon homes had been a highlight in her otherwise colorless round of days.

Most of her schooling she received at home; it was clear she couldn't keep up with Wildrose children who burst from the schoolhouse every recess and noon, in good weather, to run and romp with a vigor that seemed to anticipate the snowbound days of winter. And to struggle over sled-rutted roads in the long winter season was beyond her strength; to ride a horse was painful.

Growing into sweet young womanhood, Carolyn's days were increasingly meaningless. Although physically improved, a limp remained, and her small store of self-confidence, when she compared herself to other young women, wasn't enough to allow her into the circle of friendships she might have had otherwise.

With a show of determination that was quite unlike her, Carolyn insisted on helping "Uncles" Hubert and Harry. In spite of her mother's apprehensions she had declared, with uncharacteristic firmness, "I'm fine, Mum, much stronger than you think I am. And I need something to do—something for *me*. And at the same time, I'll be helping the uncles."

Over Regina's flutterings and hoverings, once a week Carolyn climbed on a horse and went to tackle the monumental job of bringing order out of the Runyon household's chaos. As time allowed she did some baking for them and prepared their supper before she left, tasks she had only helped with on a limited basis at home. Regina, heartbroken over what she saw as a tragedy in her precious child's life, tended to be overly solicitous, brooding over her daughter like a mother hen with one chick.

Now, in the face of that chick's flight into a world beyond the fences that had limited her, Regina fretted and stewed; it was hard to tell which bothered her more—the withdrawn child or the new independence that was revealed from time to time.

Carolyn, in her own quiet way, was showing signs of maturing into a woman with strengths never dreamed of. And she was beginning by quietly and stubbornly insisting on these trips, by herself, to a task beyond her strength.

And she thrived; her slender face, with its large, gray eyes and sensitive mouth, lost its soft formlessness and took on a firmness never hinted at previously—and never dreamed of, except perhaps by Carolyn herself.

*   *   *

Hubert swished his stick through golden wheat, gracefully bending heavy heads in the morning breeze. "Looks like it's ready," he stated. "I expect Willie'll be over tomorrow."

"You *expect!* You know he'll be over," Harry corrected scornfully. "Tomorrow's Monday, ain't it? You could set your calendar by Willie!"

"I expect I could," Hu said perversely.

"The only expectin' you do, Hu, is expectoratin'! And you can't do that too good anymore because you ain't got enough spit!"

"I expect I'll have to wrastle you to the ground," Hubert threatened amiably.

"You do, and we'll lie there until Willie comes."

"I expect you're right," Hubert said agreeably, and shambled out of reach of his brother's cane, which was weaving in his general direction. Bending stiffly, he studied the wheat. Looping his cane over one arm, he plucked a head of grain, rubbed it between his hands, and raised it to his mouth to winnow away the chaff.

"Don't blow too hard," Harry warned, "or you'll black out. You ain't got any more wind than you've got spit."

"I should let you do it, you old windbag!"

"I've been a ninny and a curmudgeon and a windbag already this morning," Harry observed with high pleasure. "Haven't lost my winnin' ways—I can see that."

Two scanty-haired heads bent over the kernels in Hu's cupped hand. "One, two, three, blow!" Harry ordered, and two withered mouths puckered and blew. The resulting hilarity was almost their undoing.

About to pop the grain into his mouth, Hu paused.

"Aha," Harry observed shrewdly. "Too many gaps in the old grinders!"

"I was just thinkin'," Hubert said, "how Virgie and Bessie always cooked up a pot of cereal out of the first wheat."

"Makes my mouth water just to think about it," Harry said, nodding. "We're not so decrepit we can't do that for ourselves. After all, we know the recipe: soak and boil."

Harry and Hubert gathered heads of ripe wheat, stuffed them in their pockets, and then the happy conspirators turned toward the house.

"Say, Hu, lookit that!"

"What, Harry?"

"They've gone and moved the house!"

"Sure have." Both men stared at the distance between them and the house; to their dim eyes and protesting legs it seemed to stretch to infinity.

The rattle of a passing rig interrupted the brothers' sounds of dismay, and they turned toward the road to watch and to wave.

"Looks like the Jameson outfit." There was a note of surprise in Harry's voice.

"Sure does. And it looks like two people in the buggy."

"Sure does. Is one of them a woman, can you tell?"

"I think so, unless some man's wearin' pink. Anyway, it has to be Dora. Jamie'd never go off to church without her."

"Must be months since they went last."

"Longer than that for us. Why in tarnation didn't we go when we had the legs to do it?"

"Didn't have the heart for it," Harry said regretfully. "We always left religion up to Virgie and Bessie. Can't depend on them now. Got to stand on our own two feet—and kneel on our own two knees."

"Harry," Hu asked thoughtfully, "do you think we'll ever get to church again?"

"Once, Hu," Harry's answer was somber. "One more time, I'd say. Now, are you ready?"

Hubert turned startled eyes on his brother. "What do you mean—ready?"

"Why, ready to go home."

"Home? What do you mean—home?" Hubert was immobilized, his eyes fixed on his brother's face, his mouth agape.

"You've heard of home, Hu. To be precise, that house back there. Quit stallin', and get to steppin', or we'll never make it by nap time. And close your mouth, Hu."

Both men were unusually quiet as they made their slow way homeward. Perhaps they needed their meager supply of strength just to navigate. Perhaps their thoughts were—finally, seriously, longingly—of another Home, and its proximity.

Indoors at last, Harry shed his sweater with a great deal of effort, and the two men puttered around the kitchen, separating the precious wheat from the chaff, putting the grain to soak in a pot of water, and cleaning up the straw that had drifted far and wide.

Finally they turned weary steps toward the other room and their rocking chairs. In spite of the mild autumn weather, a small fire burned low in the wood heater. Pulling off boots with a great deal of huffing and puffing, Harry and Hubert leaned back and stretched wooly feet toward the warmth. Hu's eyes closed.

"Hold on, Hu," Harry said with some urgency, "we've got some thinkin' to do."

"What, again?"

Harry pursued his thought: "We've got to do something about our problem."

Hu nodded; he didn't need it spelled out. "You're sayin' we can't make it much longer alone."

"That's it. We can't make it through another winter by ourselves. Good as Willie is, and Caro too, it isn't enough. We're alone most of the time, to take care of things that's gettin' too much for us, like gettin' the wood into the house from the woodpile, emptying the slops, fixin' meals. Our cookin' alone is going to kill us!"

"And one of us," Hu said grimly, "has got to go in there soon and fix dinner. It ain't a pleasin' prospect."

"Face it, Hu: one day we'll wake up dead!"

In heavy silence the brothers faced the reality of their situation: alone, aged, infirm, no children or grandchildren, no place to go.

"So what are we going to do, Harry?" Hubert, as in days long past, looked to his older brother.

"There's only one solution that I can see—get someone to live here with us."

"Good idea. You handle it, Harry." Hu put his head back and closed his eyes. But he opened them at Harry's silence, fraught with meaning, and asked uneasily, "Any ideas, Harry?"

"Not a one."

"I guess it's prayin' time, Harry."

"You want to do it?"

"You go head, Harry. I'll chime in if you don't get it right."

From a small isolated spot beside a low fire in a rude house, surrounded by endless miles of bush, two old men folded work-worn hands, bowed stiff necks, and lifted the thin sound of earnest prayer: *"God, You did such a good job when You sent Willie Tucker to take care of our fields, and Caro to take care of our house. And we thank You for it* [unaccustomed amens from Hu]. *But now, it seems, we need help again. We're in a real pickle, Lord, on account of You've left us here so long, and we're so helpless . . ."*

"He knows all that, Harry! Ask Him what you're gonna ask Him!"

"Good thing the Lord's got more patience than you, Hu. Now gimme a chance." Harry's querulous tones changed to earnestness again as he continued, *"Lord, have You got someone who could come live with us? Perhaps someone who needs us as bad as we need them? We'd like that, Lord."*

"Amen!"

And Hubert and Harry put their heads back for their naps with lighter hearts than they had known for a long time. After all, their prayer record was perfect thus far: One prayer, one answer. It was good ground for faith.

*A*s she had settled down to life in the bush, one of the first things Abbie understood was the need for human contact that drove a homesteader to the window whenever a rig passed by. Whether buggy, wagon, surrey, or cart in the summer, or cutter or sleigh in the winter, the jingle of the harness and the rattle of the rig meant people. Women, confined to the house as they were, bore the brunt of the loneliness, the sense of isolation that was one of the keenest hardships of pioneer life, and Abbie quickly found she was no exception.

To catch sight of another living, loving, struggling, crying, laughing, lonely person eased for her the sense of being adrift on some endless green sea.

At first it had seemed rude to be caught pulling back a curtain and peering at passersby. But she experienced for herself the disappointment of passing a house from which there was no visible sign of humanity and no wave, that silent expression of camaraderie. Wordless, the wave spoke volumes. "I'm here," it said, "and I'm here for you."

When, struggling with the buttons on Merry's Sunday shoes and concluding she would need to get into the shed soon and search for a larger size, Abbie heard the faint sounds that could only mean someone was driving past, she turned to the window, pulled back the flocked curtain, and unabashedly, waved. Sure enough, the face of the man in the buggy was turned toward the house, and he waved, warming Abbie's heart. Her next glimpse was of the woman at his side—taut, stiff, unresponsive; the face, shaded by a large-brimmed hat, stared straight ahead.

"Who was that, Mum?" Cameron called from the small bedroom he shared with his twin. Half in and half out of his drawers, he hopped to the doorway and turned curious eyes on his mother.

"Go back and finish dressing," Abbie told her son, "we're running late. It's the neighbors, and you'll see them at church."

"The Jamesons?" Worth asked, lifting an eyebrow.

Abbie nodded. "Going to church, I guess, after all this time."

"I've met James—Jamie, they call him—several times. Nice fellow. But I've never so much as seen the wife. Dora, isn't it? And you haven't seen much of her, if I have the story right."

"I certainly won't recognize her. Although I'll never forget that eye . . ."

"Funny lady," small Merry said brightly.

"No, love," Abbie said, kneeling swiftly at her daughter's side to finish buttoning her shoes. "She's sick."

"Funny," Merry insisted, and Abbie didn't challenge her. Certainly Dora had acted both sick *and* funny when Abbie and Merry had gone to call.

Abbie knew that Dora was considered to be "strange" since the death of her sons, but she had been assured Dora also had good days. In the throes of coming to terms with her own loneliness, Abbie's heart had gone out to the unseen neighbor, wrapped in her secret sorrow, and when she had a comparatively free afternoon, she and Merry had taken a leisurely walk down the road to the Jameson place.

Clutching a bouquet of wildflowers they had gathered along the way—a fragrant offer of friendship—they had turned in at the gate and Abbie chilled again at the utter cheerlessness of the scene. Her own yard was full of activity and sound: children at play or work, animals scurrying at their heels; Worth endlessly busy, and usually whistling; creatures, both wild and tame, singing and crowing and cackling and bawling and squealing.

Here, she knew, there were no children—now; the sad fact seemed to leech color and life from everything.

The muffled sound of hammering from one of the outbuildings was an encouragement. Abbie and Merry quickened their pace through the dust of the lane and turned toward the house. The door was slightly ajar, and it opened a few more inches from the force of Abbie's knock.

The silence seemed to throb; instinct told her that someone was there. She was dismayed to feel the back of her neck prickle.

Abbie hesitated. As she was about to turn and leave, a faint shuffling sound caught her attention. Feet, perhaps slippered, reached the door and halted. By now half mesmerized, Abbie clutched Merry's hand and fixed her eyes on the narrow opening.

A thin hand with long, untended nails, appeared, grasping the edge of the door. A wisp of unkempt hair came into sight, then one ear—a cheek—an eye. The eye, dull and lifeless, stared unblinkingly at Abbie.

"Hello," Abbie managed, and felt that her smile was a caricature. "I'm your new neighbor, Abigail Rooney, and this is Merry, my daughter."

The one-eyed gaze lowered to the child at Abbie's side; the face—what Abbie could see of it—flinched. A terrible desolation seemed to settle over the half-exposed countenance, sweeping aside the blankness and giving a glimpse of feelings so painful as to be unendurable. Abbie felt as though a curtain had been ripped aside momentarily and sanity looked out, but a sanity too terrible to be borne. Sanity fled and emptiness returned; the face withdrew as slowly as it had appeared, half-inch by half-inch, until the eye was gone, the cheek, the ear, the wisp of hair. All that remained was the clawlike hand gripping the door.

Abbie's bright remarks had died unuttered in her throat, and Merry's smile was uncertain. Speaking to the empty space, Abbie said gently, "We're going now." Laying the flowers on top of an empty cream can, she and Merry retreated down the lane to the road.

If she hadn't cast a last glance over her shoulder, she would have missed seeing the slight figure that slipped from the doorway to the flowers, snatched them up, clutched them to her scrawny bosom, and disappeared into the house.

Jamie Jameson had stopped by the Rooney place a time or two, always alone and always in a hurry to leave, refusing Worth's invitation to come in and get acquainted. Whether or not he knew of her visit to his wife, Abbie never knew.

Now, passing by, he waved, and Abbie wondered if her response brought any measure of cheer to the lonely man with the lonelier woman at his side.

Worth went to harness the horse and hitch it to the buggy, and Abbie returned to the task of getting her children— healthy, happy, *here*, she thought fervently—ready for church, touching them when she didn't need to, straightening clothes that hung perfectly, caressing rosy cheeks, and fondling heads of thick, fair hair until finally the boys, impatient at what they felt was too much coddling, frowned and pulled away. The very naturalness of the boyish reaction swelled her heart with thanksgiving for her blessings.

When Worth called from the yard, the children ran for the waiting rig, and Abbie paused long enough to fire the

kitchen range, close the damper, and pop a roasting pan into the oven; with luck, their dinner would be ready when
they got home.

She shooed both cats outside and pulled the door shut
behind her (there were no locked doors in the bush). And
then it was up into the "Jim-Dandy Jump Seat Buggy" for
a spin down the road, through the bright sunshine under a
cloudless sky, with a pleasant expectation of meeting new
friends and neighbors for a carefree hour or two—and to
worship, Abbie tagged on hastily.

Today there were very few watching faces along the
route; almost everyone, it seemed, was taking advantage of
the year's last few glorious days before chill north winds
swept down, reminding them of a bitter winter ahead
when travel would be difficult, gatherings few, and loneliness a thing to be reckoned with.

Today loneliness was laid aside as, down numerous
paths, newly made trails, and a few roads, the good people
of Wildrose turned thoughts and hearts toward the little
white schoolhouse at the center of the community.

For the homesteader, the school building played a big
part; it provided a community meeting place. Socials, po-
litical meetings, picnics, musical "concerts" (most boasted
an organ or piano), and, of course, church services were all
held in it. Everybody attended, young and old. Without a
doubt, the schoolhouse was an oasis in a wide, lonely land.

As the Rooneys progressed along the country road—
the children scrubbed and brushed to within an inch of
their lives, bouncing on the spring seat, and Worth,
debonair in his Sunday suit of dark gray vicuna, at her
side—Abbie's dark fears receded a little. Recalling her early-morning prayer, she renewed her resolve and hoped
fleetingly that the minister's message might offer courage.

"Look!" shrieked Merry from Abbie's lap, her small
finger pointing. "There's Caro!"

The Morris wagon was turning into the road ahead of them. The Rooney tribe waved and the children shouted greetings until Worth hushed them.

"Caro didn't see me," Merry complained, disappointed. Carolyn Morris was one of her favorite grown-ups.

Caro, it seemed to Abbie, was interested elsewhere. Approaching the Morris wagon was a high-stepping horse and what seemed, even at this distance, an equally arrogant rider. It could be none other than Micah Lille, little known (except by reputation) to Abbie. She watched as, passing the Morris family, the handsome métis nodded a greeting. In their usual friendly way, Samuel, Collum, and Regina nodded, perhaps spoke; Carolyn sat as one transfixed. Even after the man had passed, the young girl watched until her head turned to accommodate her scrutiny. Finally, it seemed to Abbie, Regina gave a swift look back, turned, said something to her daughter, and Carolyn swung around.

When Micah Lille passed the Rooneys, Abbie had her first close look at the notorious half-breed. Son of Joe and Ruby Lille, who were farmers like the rest of the community—and fine people, by all counts—Micah was something of an enigma. He spent more time in the north, probably on the reservation with his full-blooded brothers, than he did at home. No doubt he was here to assist his father with the harvest.

As buggy and horseman met, dark eyes burned into Abbie's before the proud head, black hair falling around his bronzed cheeks like a cascade, bent in a nod. No smile curved what was probably the handsomest mouth Abbie had ever seen—full, shapely. Cruel? "Don't be fanciful!" Abbie scolded herself, aware that the earlier settlers' fears of the Indians had left an understandable uneasiness in those who followed.

But even the children were affected. Indians, particularly those of mixed blood, were commonplace, and the twins, as they hunkered back in the jump seat, were more awestruck than anything. Abbie could almost predict that on the morrow the boys would be whittling arrows and fastening arrowheads to them that had been turned up by the plow, fashioning bows, and whooping and hollering as they chased their sister, chicken feathers stuck in a band on their heads.

Unlike Carolyn, Abbie had no desire to turn and follow the enigmatic man on the spirited horse, unlike the plow horses of the area's farms as the nobleman was unlike the farmers.

"Caro better be careful," she muttered, half to herself, partly to Worth. "A man like that could eat her alive."

"Hon," Worth scoffed, "a man like that wouldn't give a mouse like Caro the time of day. Can you imagine an eagle courting a sparrow?"

"No," Abbie said thoughtfully, "but I can imagine an eagle destroying a sparrow."

5

*A*bbie herded the children into the building while Worth went to find a spot to tie the horse and buggy. Among the rigs piling up in the clearing, the "Jim-Dandy Jump Seat Buggy" stood out like a thoroughbred among scrubs. Abbie, fearful that it gave them a status they didn't deserve, was uncomfortable in the face of the decrepit wagons and worn buggies from which equally workworn men and women were alighting.

If you only knew, she thought, looking around. Of all of you I'm the weakest, the most unsure. And our finances . . . Abbie considered their shrunken funds grimly and regretted the picture of affluence they presented when they were, in fact, as dependent for survival on the harvest as any of them.

But the handshakes were genuine, the smiles open, and Abbie's heart warmed as the stalwart people of the bush pressed around, greeting one another as brother to brother and sister to sister.

No matter that hands were calloused, faces sunbaked. No matter that haircuts were amateurish and necks gleamed white under recent barberings. No matter that long arms stuck awkwardly out of sleeves grown too short, or that hand-me-downs bunched large on small forms. No matter that dresses were faded, hats had seen better days. No matter that barn smells lingered on patched footgear. When the opening strains of "O God, Our Help in Ages Past" wheezed from the old organ and heavy-booted and Sunday-slippered feet stood for the first hymn of the day, a glory seemed to settle over the little building as the week's problems were laid aside, and heart joined heart in praise of a power that had not failed "in ages past" and was indeed "hope for years to come."

For Abbie, the words "Under the shadow of Thy throne/Still may we dwell secure;/Sufficient is Thine arm alone,/And our defense is sure," was more a prayer than a song. Almost—almost—could she believe it true in this atmosphere of faith?

Her own needs were forgotten, though, when with the force of a blow, certain words in the hymn lifted from the throats of the worshipers and Abbie's eyes encountered a face as pain-filled as any she had ever seen. The song whispered out on her lips at the stark misery of the man Jamie Jameson.

Standing at the side of the slight, empty-faced woman, the man couldn't have looked any more stricken if an arrow had pierced his heart. "Time, like an ever-rolling stream," the group sang, "Bears all its sons away;/They fly, forgotten, as a dream/Dies at the op'ning day."

The singers, to whom the Jameson tragedy was an old one, seemed not to note the song's application; the song leader had no knowledge that today Jamie and Dora would be in the service. Abbie, to whom the painful story was new, felt a surge of compassion for the bereaved pair.

But she might as well have saved her sympathy for Dora; the woman seemed untouched, lost perhaps in her distant world where little, if anything, was allowed in, least of all anything painful.

The hymn singing completed, the group, with a great deal of clattering, heaving, and squeezing, seated itself. As the service proceeded, Abbie tuned out, lost in sympathy as she looked for the first time at the broken woman.

Dora Jameson's untidy hair was caught back in a knot; her skin was sallow and her body painfully thin. She was motionless and expressionless, except that her bony fingers twisted a button on the bodice of her faded pink cotton dress until Abbie wondered if she would worry it completely off.

James—or Jamie, as everyone called him—was a big man, with wiry dark hair, a square jaw emphasized by the way he continually clenched the muscles in it, and gentle eyes—gentle, shadowed eyes. Abbie sighed and looked away. Perhaps, knowing a little of their story, she was imagining things that weren't so.

Jamie Jameson shifted his position in the narrow confines of a seat not intended to accommodate a man of his size and made an effort to bring his thoughts into some semblance of order. The hymn, with its reference to "sons," had badly shaken the walls against hurt that he so painstakingly built and rebuilt. Dora's walls were impregnable; sometimes he envied her the pain-free existence she lived behind them.

It had been a struggle to get to church, but he felt it was important that they come. It had been a long time since he attempted it, and he probably wouldn't try it throughout the long winter.

Here, in an atmosphere of faith, it was easier to look for the miracle that would bring light back to his wife's eyes. Most of the time he felt it would never happen, but in church, with a certain measure of peace seeping into his soul and an unspoken prayer swelling his heart, hope stirred.

With his decision made, he had started early with the things he had to do. Outside chores completed, he had fixed breakfast, encouraged Dora to eat, as he always had to do, and cleared up the table while she sat in her chair looking out the window. He piled the dishes in a pan of water and left them on the back of the range; he'd do them later.

However often he ironed, Jamie always felt awkward about it. Having padded the tabletop and heated the iron, though, he did his best to get the wrinkles from a dress that had been in a ball in the bottom of the closet for goodness knew how long. In the matter of Dora's grooming and personal appearance, Jamie felt particularly helpless. And Dora was no help. She allowed him to slip the dress on her, button it, and submitted to his efforts to comb some of the tangles from her hair. Holding a mirror up in front of her, he asked, "How does it look, Dorrie? Can you fix it a little better? Come on—that's my girl."

But he knew before he tried that there would be no answer, not today. This was one of her silent days. *My God!* he prayed. *The torture of the silences!* Better the harsh recriminations her befuddled mind heaped on him at times than to bear the silences. For in the silences he knew she had blanked out what she couldn't bear to face and escaped him completely.

"Dorrie," he had said patiently, after the horse and buggy were at the door, "put on your hat now. Let's go." When she turned empty eyes on him, he explained again, "It's Sunday, Dorrie. We're going to church. You'll see Regina today. You'll like that, won't you?"

At times it aroused a flicker of response when Regina Morris's name was mentioned. For it had been Regina who had seen her through those dark days during his absence when death lurked in the shadows reaching greedy hands for her, having already snatched the breath from the throats of her children. And he not there!

God! he prayed for the ten-thousandth time. *Forgive!* It just might be that divine love would indeed forgive. But human love—never. As living proof, his wife sat by his side wrapped in a sickness of sorrow, a madness of hate.

There was little he could do but pray. And Jamie bowed his head and prayed.

"The path of the just is as the shining light," expounded Brother Victor, reading from the Bible in his hand.

"We came here today by many paths," he said. "Some took shortcuts, some chose dusty roads, some came on unbroken trails. Some drove behind horses, a few came on horseback, many walked.

"For some it was a tiring trip. Others made it on strong, quick legs. Some came willingly, others were prodded, coaxed, or," with a smile, "ordered to come [self-conscious wiggles among the restless young people]. Some came solely for the purpose of meeting a special person [sly jabs in the ribs of the young men in the back of the room]. A few even came to meet a very special Person." A meaningful glance upward added a humorous but significant emphasis.

The similarity of their physical trek and their spiritual journey was the theme of the hour. No matter how arduous the path or how dark the way, "God, who commanded the light to shine out of darkness, hath shined in our hearts." No one, the man of God said, with the light of God in his heart, is ever truly in darkness.

For Jamie, the message rang emptily on his ears and on his bruised heart. The "shining light" seemed as far removed from his own dark path as day from night.

As so often happened, the help Jamie came to find evaded him. Today it was because the shining light was, obviously, for the pathway of the just; Jamie numbered himself with the unjust. For without a doubt he had been at fault in his responsibility to Dora and the boys.

And yet, if he had the decision to make again, the decision that had proved so disastrous, how could he do other than he had done? God knew he hadn't wanted to leave his wife and children, isolated and alone, in a bush country winter. But in the face of their desperate financial need, what choice did he have? What choice did many of the other men of the district have? When the crop had failed, they had done what they had to do to provide for their families. Some had worked in the north woods, others in the gristmill in Prince Albert, and a few had gone all the way to the coast to find work. In all cases it was away from Wildrose, and transportation was undependable as trains were held up because of snowstorms and schedules were meaningless. A man could not count on getting home and back in a weekend. So whatever he did, it was bound to be a long haul, both for him as worker and the wife as waiter.

"Don't go, Jamie!" Dora had pleaded when he first mentioned it. "We'll manage some way, if you're here. Without you . . ."

"Dorrie," Jamie pleaded, "please don't make this any harder for me than it is. You can't think I want to go. But what else can I do? We simply can't make it through until spring with the food we have on hand. We need cash for so many things!"

"Work in Meridian, then!"

"Where, Dora?"

When she couldn't answer that, knowing as well as he the tiny hamlet with its one store, post office, barber shop, and smithy, her eyes had searched the room for something of worth. What could they do without? The stove, table and chairs, a couple of rocking chairs, an old buffet, their dishes and cookware all were things they needed and of little or no worth to anyone else. And besides, who had money to buy them? The horses and the cow were essential if they were to continue farming; there was nothing to sell.

Jamie had waited as long as he felt he could. Finally he had climbed, grim-faced, from the trap door in the floor.

"There are enough potatoes to see us through another month," he reported. "There are two cabbages, a sack of onions, probably half a box of carrots, and they're withering. The turnips are about done, the chickens aren't laying enough to help, and the few eggs down there in the bin are getting watery."

"There are canned things, Jamie!" Dora said desperately.

Jamie had an exact count. "Eight quarts of beans. Four of peas. Some wild fruit, and most of it without sugar. What's the flour situation?" Knowing, she wouldn't say.

When she hadn't answered, biting her lips, Jamie strode to the cupboard. The hundred-pound sack was half empty. Sugar, tea, even dried beans—when the present supply was gone, how would they replace them? You could charge only so much if you ever wanted to get free!

In a silence that was to become heartbreakingly familiar, Dora watched her husband's preparations to go. Jamie chopped and stacked enough wood to last a month. He pulled hay from the corners of the barn loft toward the trap door so that it could be forked easily to the floor below. He showed the boys how to strip the cow of the little milk she was giving, how to break the ice in the trough, how to mix mash for the hens.

He scraped the stalls clean and reminded the boys to spread clean straw during the week; he arranged for young Collum Morris to come once a week and muck out the barn. The team he would take to the Morrises until he returned.

On the last morning he cleaned the grate in the range and carried out the ashes; he shoveled a path through the new-fallen snow to the outbuildings and the woodpile. He piled the woodbox to overflowing and stacked an extra supply of firewood on the porch. And then they heard the jingle of approaching horses and the hearty call of the men in the sleigh.

"I'll try and get back every month or so," he said to the woman standing there, rigid and frigid, in silence. "Dorrie . . . ," he pleaded, but her eyes were shuttered; she fixed them in contemplation of the faded linoleum. Neither did she say the words that would have freed him from the torment that was to pursue him across the years.

When he reached for her, she turned her cheek for his kiss, her face clouded with the bitterness that was to consume her, and her lips were denied him in the decision that was to last longer than she could have known.

Jamie put on his worn sheep-lined duck coat, picked up his bag, touched a finger to the rosy cheeks of his sons, rumpled their dark heads, and left.

Three years later, sitting under a sermon intended to offer courage and hope, Jamie Jameson felt the ceaseless contortions of the fingers of the woman at his side were twisting his very insides, and he clenched the muscles of his jaws until they ached.

With the crop in, Wildrose embarked on its most exciting time of the year, aside from Christmas. With bills paid first and a careful assessment of the year's needs taken into consideration, the remaining cash (if any) and the possibilities it offered sent almost palpable waves of bliss from one side of the district to the other.

Having been deprived of all but basic necessities most of the year, and these usually in short supply, the isolated homesteader turned to the catalog as avidly as plow horses seek a watering trough at the close of a long day's labor.

Common sense prevailed: worn clothes were replaced, footwear ordered, along with rifle cartridges, felt boots, hog scrapers, gauntlets, galvanized pails, knitting yarns, crochet cotton, darning cotton.

Women pored over the black-and-white pictures of material of all kinds, agonizing over quality and color: gingham for aprons, flannel for sleepwear, muslin for drawers, cheesecloth for dairy products, and sheeting—bleached if you could afford the extra two pennies a yard, unbleached if you couldn't. In that case, you did your own bleaching, spreading the coarse ecru yardage across the yard, over low bushes (safe from wandering chickens), until it turned "nice and white" as promised.

It was the time to buy bed ticking, cotton batting, mosquito netting (for window screens), gopher traps, chamber pots, water dippers, tea steepers, coffee boilers, milk skimmers. It was time to order the yearly oilcloth for the table, and perhaps a colorful linoleum for the rough board floor. It was time to replenish shoe blacking, tooth soap, brilliantine.

With medical care unavailable, it was a time of ordering "Soda Mint Tablets" for sour stomach, flatulency, and nausea; "Bronchial Troches" for coughs, colds, sore throats, and hoarseness; "Pepsin Tablets" for dyspepsia and indigestion; and "Compound Licorice Powder," a laxative ("children take it readily").

It was time for a few foolish fancies. John Mobley fulfilled a secret dream by ordering "Pomade Philacome," an "exquisite dressing for the hair and mustache." His brother Leroy opted for "Olive Wax Pomatum" to "fix and layer the hair, whiskers, and mustache." Norma, their sister and almost as mustachioed as her brothers and as eager to be free of hair as John and Leroy were to cultivate it, ordered the "Famous Parisian Depilatory." This nostrum, she was assured, "instantly dissolves hair wherever applied, removing it entirely and forever." Hair on the "face, neck, or arms, so embarrassing to ladies of refinement, can now be removed without danger or chance of failure." Talk about miracles!

Grandma Dunphy's family banded together and ordered her a "Black Japanned Hearing Horn." Tom Brewster, with rhythm in his soul, ordered rosewood bones, and his son Tommy, following in the musical footsteps of his father, ordered for 13 cents a harmonica with 10 double holes on each edge and 80 reeds. Winter, in the Brewster household, would be filled with toe-tapping sound.

Daisy Chalmers, at a loss concerning sharing the facts of life with her three lively, curious boys (and their father too tongue-tied to talk about it), sent for *True Manhood*, a "manual of science and guide to health, strength, and purity, revealing physiological facts and uncovering truths with a chaste and gentle hand." This work, she was promised, "is devoted to the presentation of facts which are eagerly sought by all boys verging upon manhood."

Of the orders trickling steadily out of the homes of the bush, perhaps the items they did not contain were more telling than the items ordered. Though fascinating, everyone scorned the "Magic Flesh Builder and Cupper," with its amazing promise to "permanently remove wrinkles and make sunken cheeks smooth." "Obesity Powders," for lean Wildrose homesteaders, were unnecessary. Metallic hens' nests, "recommended by poultry raisers everywhere," were considered an extravagance for Wildrose chickens. No female spent her small allowance on ventilated dress and corset protectors, ostrich neck boas, or silk-lined mocha gloves. No male seriously considered a celluloid shirt front, "fancy random figured underwear," or all-silk suspenders of "assorted light colors and the daintiest of patterns." Wildrose funds, hard to come by, were not spent casually.

The most peculiar order, snickered over in many a Wildrose household, was Peter Smiley's grass suit. Made of "long tough marsh grass" into a cape coat with hood, guaranteed waterproof and easily packed and carried, Peter looked like a small haystack when hunched in it at the lake's edge. Moreover, it frightened away the wild geese and ducks he was stalking.

A most envied purchase was, undoubtedly, Mona Byers' work-saving appliance, the "Peerless Wringer." With its clamping device, guide roller, and double gears, it would revolutionize washday in one Wildrose household.

* * *

In the log house with its faded red door, Hubert and Harry Runyon pulled chairs up to the old oak table, spread the "wish book" in front of them, and turned the pages with thick fingers until they located the item of their choice.

"Shall we get spectacles, or eyeglasses?" asked Hu, peering through the magnifying glass at the page of eye wear.

"Here, gimme that glass," Harry said testily, "so I can make up our minds. I like these 'Riding Bow Spectacles' myself."

"I like the 'Straight Temple Spectacles,'" Hu declared. "That way we can tell 'em apart."

"It says," Harry read, "not to get the cheap grades; they're almost certain to do untold injury to the eyes."

"They're warranteed for 10 years, Harry! Unless we're buried in 'em, we won't get our money's worth."

They moved on to "Instructions for Testing the Eyes" and its numerous questions. Never certain of their ages, Hu bypassed that question by printing, "Younger than my brother." Harry, not to be outdone, laboriously printed, "Older than my brother."

The question "Do your eyes stand out prominently or are they sunken?" brought the brothers nose to nose to study each other critically, lick their pencils, and write, "Yes."

When they came to the question dealing with the smallest print they could read, and at what distance, with much ado they held the chart for each other, moving it back and forth until they determined their present vision.

"I can see the *O P* line," Hu reported, while Harry could see only the big *E* clearly.

"Now," Harry said, studying the questions through the reading glass, "they want to know the distance between pupils."

"They sit pretty close together in Wildrose school," Hu said, scratching his head, "but why does that matter?"

"In your eyes, ignoramus! How close together are your eyes?"

"I can't see my own eyes," Hu complained, resulting in more close studying of each other's face. "Say, Harry, you sure got big pores!" he exclaimed, letting the magnifying glass roam over his brother's seamed face.

Harry snatched the glass from Hu's hand and returned to a study of the questions. "Number 10," he read. "What is the width of your nose at the base?"

"My problem ain't with my nose, Harry," Hu objected. "I can breathe perfect. It's my eyes is givin' me trouble. You sure you got the right page? Maybe you're ordering handkerchiefs."

"They have to fit the spectacles to your nose, Hu," Harry said patiently and guessed at two inches, while Hu printed "Wider than before I read the question."

"One more," Harry said with a sigh of relief. "How wide are you at the temples?"

"Wider'n you, Harry."

With a great deal of wrangling—the finest they'd been able to work up in days—the order was completed. Well satisfied, Hu settled back in his chair. Harry turned to a marked page, cleared his throat, and said, "Hu."

"Huh?" Hubert was quickly (for him) alert. Perhaps the day's repartee wasn't finished after all.

"When we're sending this order, we better think ahead to next winter and get us some remedies. Remember the aches and pains and coughs and sniffles we came up with?"

"Came down with, you mean."

"Here's a kit with 36 bottles in it. Seems to me, though, we don't need medicine for some of these things." Harry let the glass roam over the list. "We ain't never had a sign of epilepsy or St. Vitus' dance. And we don't need a

cure for seasickness, or bilious colic, or salt rheum erup-
tions."

"Maybe we've got them and don't know."

"We can make our own selection of 12 remedies, Hu,
for $1.50, and they'll send a free instruction sheet. Now
let's see . . ."

"Adults take six pellets from two to four doses every
day," Hu spelled out over his brother's shoulder. "That
should keep us busy most of the winter."

Laboriously, the brothers chose 12 cures, including
toothache, nervous debility, dropsy and fluid accumula-
tions, catarrh, influenza and cold in the head, dyspepsia,
indigestion, and weak stomach.

"It's wonderful, ain't it, what medical science has
come up with?" the brothers marveled.

"I don't feel easy about these order numbers," Harry
said. "I think we better have Caro check them for us when
she comes tomorrow."

"That's right—she's comin' tomorrow, ain't she?" The
thought was enough to send Hu, pleased with the day's
activities, back to his chair and his nap with happy anticipation of good times yet to come.

"Willie comes the day after Caro," he figured. "We're
gettin' to be regular social butterflies." He fell asleep re-
gretting Harry hadn't heard that remark; Hu couldn't
imagine what in the world he might have come up with. It
might have precipitated another whole round of palaver.

* * *

Roaney, the Morrises' old plow horse, lumbered ponderously along the road, his passenger, no heavier than a
feather, straddling his wide back.

On her weekly trip to the "uncles," Carolyn rode bare-
back, reins slack in her hand, luxuriating in Roaney's
warmth on her thighs and the autumn sun's gentle

warmth on her slight shoulders and slim arms. Her fine, flyaway hair moved only slightly in the small breeze the horse's progress created.

It was good to be out; it was rapture to be alone, to absorb the ambience of the bush—its special fragrances, its spectrum of fall colors, the exhilarating freshness of its air. The bush held no fears for Carolyn Morris, who was born and raised in Wildrose. It was beauty, it was safety, it was *home.* Much as she loved her family—father, mother, brother—she often felt smothered by their protectiveness. But she understood it.

Carolyn had been a lively, happy, outgoing child of eight when she had fallen from the tree, injuring her back severely. Bedridden for months, screaming with pain when she was moved, she had slowly mended. But the long inactivity had weakened one leg, probably shortening it a little, and she was left with a residual discomfort that had faded slightly with the passing of the years. Her family's compassion kept them hovering over her protectively, smotheringly. Her activities were greatly curtailed as her family constantly urged her to be careful, to rest, not to overdo.

Young womanhood found Carolyn subdued, obedient, gentle. "Poor Caro," people were prone to say. "So limited, missing out on everything. And really rather pretty in a pale, quiet way. I wonder what the future can hold for her?"

But somewhere underneath the patina of resignation, the mildness, the submission smoldered the fires of independence, passion, vigor, and a quiet strength that would have astonished anyone glimpsing the unquenched flame.

Her emergence from helplessness to hope wasn't fully recognized even by Carolyn. But her weekly trips to the Runyon household, undertaken against the cautions of her parents, were evidences of that struggle for freedom. It was true that Harry and Hubert needed help and needed it desperately, but in her insistence that she could ride to their place by herself and was strong enough to do the work, Carolyn tasted an independence that was heady for one so long deprived of it.

Now she lifted the hem of her skirt, stretched her weak leg, twisting it experimentally and watching its near-normal function critically. She was, consequently, unprepared when a high-stepping horse pulling a swaying buggy burst from an opening in the bush on her left, careening into the road and tilting dangerously in its tight swing to avoid the plodding horse.

"Oh, my goodness!" Carolyn gasped, as Roaney, startled, lunged ponderously, and she felt herself begin to slide from the massive back. Clutching futilely at the mane, she tumbled in a heap to the ground.

More shaken than hurt, more embarrassed than angry, she heard, with some dim part of her, a man's urgent voice controlling an alarmed horse, followed by rapid footsteps. Kneeling at her side, he made a low sound of dismay, and Carolyn felt herself half-lifted as his arm went under her shoulders.

Stunned by the speed with which it had all happened, Carolyn blinked, focused her eyes, and looked into the face of Micah Lille.

Micah's dark eyes, which she had always considered unfathomable, were filled with concern. His face, which she had always seen as proud, was bent over her solicitously. The handsome mouth had lost its chiseled arrogancy.

Cradled against his shoulder, Carolyn's hand went automatically to the half-breed's chest, and her eyes, only inches from his, studied—for the time it took that strong heart beneath her palm to beat a dozen times—the strong face and saw it open, without affectation, vulnerable and real.

"Are you hurt?" the deep voice questioned anxiously.

Belatedly aware of her disarrayed clothing, Carolyn tugged ineffectively at her skirts in an effort at modesty. Somehow, she feared, it was too late for that. And her hair! Too late to worry about that too; pins had come loose, and fair wisps curled on her shoulders and across her cheeks.

"Do you really think you should stand up?" the man asked, as Carolyn, wincing but determined, got to her feet. But not without Micah Lille's supporting arm.

"I'm fine," she managed as firmly as possible and never knew a quaver in her voice betrayed the fright she had felt. She moved from the circle of his arm and never knew a tremble told the lie of her independence.

"I'm fine," she insisted, and never knew how pathetic her brave effort seemed in the face of her frailty.

"I can see that," the man said gently.

"If you'll help me back on," she said, dusting her skirt and looking around for Roaney, "I'll appreciate it."

Micah Lille brought Roaney from the side of the road where he was placidly cropping grass. Spanning her waist with his two hands, he swung her up onto the horse's back and placed the reins in her unsteady hands.

"Are you sure . . . ," he began.

Carolyn's chin lifted. "I'm sure."

The man stood silently at her side, studying her face, his eyes once again inscrutable. But looking down into Micah Lille's face, Carolyn realized she would never again see his eyes as remote, she would never again see his face as haughty, his mouth would never seem scornful to her again.

She urged Roaney forward and never knew that Micah Lille watched as she rode away, until, with a shake of his shoulders—as though freeing himself from some threatened bond—he bounded up into the buggy, startled the horse with a harsh command, and spun down the road.

*I*ndian summer, that lazy link between autumn and winter, had lingered too long. Reluctant as they were to let it go, the people of Wildrose recognized all too soon the frigid fingers and chilling breath of the "long season." It was ushered in by none other than Jack Frost himself, who crept about during the night now, spangling Mother Nature's bosom with shimmering jewels, only to retreat briefly when the sun pulled itself, ever slower and lower, over the horizon in the morning.

Now the homesteaders of the bush allowed themselves a breathing spell, a brief moment between the hustle and bustle of the summer and the enforced hibernation of the winter. Oh, there was plenty to do—wood to haul, saw, chop, and stack; fodder to prepare; chinking to do; animals to butcher; cellars to arrange and rearrange; storm windows to put up. But there was a sense of waiting, a sort of calm-before-the-storm feeling, that marked their days. Now was the time for a community get-together, a celebration of work accomplished, harvest gathered in, and winter preparations made.

Cold as it was, the lakes had not yet frozen solid, so a skating party was out of the question. Someone suggested a box supper, but that more or less excluded the children:

not every member of the family could, realistically, have money to bid on a box. And children were rarely, if ever, excluded from the district gatherings. For one thing—who would mind them? For another, what parent could endure the reproach in his child's eyes if he were left at home? No, community affairs across the Territories habitually included the entire family.

A game night was eventually decided upon. And, of course, the school was the only meeting place considered for it. Not only was its one room more spacious than any "front" room in Wildrose, but it had the added advantage of being centrally located.

Every homemaker produced the tastiest goodies of which she was capable (and which her limited pantry would allow). Rhubarb pies, butter tarts, Scotch shortbread, sponge cake, homemade candy—all were tantalizingly prepared ahead of time and kept, by constant surveillance, from sneak attacks by avid-eyed children and equally rapacious husbands. Flattering for the cook though they were, it was a matter of pride to arrive at the "doings" with her offering splendid in appearance and mouth-watering in aroma.

The Rooney wagon stopped at the Morris farm to pick up Samuel, Regina, and Carolyn; Collum Morris had gone ahead with the horse and buggy to help arrange desks and tables for the evening's activities.

With much heaving and pulling and a great deal of chaffing, rotund Regina was hoisted up over the wheel, into the wagon and seated beside Abbie on the spring seat. Carolyn climbed into the back, to settle on the floor of the rig among the blanketed children, small Merry cuddled on her lap. When Samuel climbed aboard, to stand with Worth at the front of the wagon, Worth clucked to the team, and with a jingle of harness and bone-shaking rattling, they were off.

"Keep the blankets over you," Worth cautioned the women and children as he turned up the collar of his mackinaw and turned down the band of his muskrat skin cap. "We'll soon see," he had said to Abbie with a grin when he put it on for the first time, "if it 'protects every part of the neck, side of the face, and head' as promised."

Watching him now, in the light of the lantern, Abbie had to laugh. The "extra-long visor, which, when turned down, affords protection to front of the face," undeniably did just what it promised. Between the visor and the collar, Worth's cheerful face grinned back. "Owing to the rush of the northern climates," the catalog had advised, "a desirable cap to exclude the cold is a necessity."

Still showing what greenhorns we are, Abbie thought, glancing at Samuel's worn ear-flapped cap, tied snugly under his chin.

But the "rush of the northern climate" was a reality tonight. The weak warmth of the day had been quickly overtaken by a chill wind. Occasional clouds scudded across a full moon, and Sam said he wouldn't be surprised to see snow before morning; there was a definite feel of winter in the air.

Abbie thought of Brother Victor's Sunday scripture: "The harvest is past, the summer is ended." Although he had made a spiritual application, the words had rung in Abbie's heart in a somber way: The good weather is over . . .

The sting of sleet chilled more than Abbie's face; the ghostly, bare arms of the trees seemed to reach for her, and she shrank under the protection of the quilt. Merry's voice, shrilling a question to "Aunt Gina," recalled Abbie to normalcy.

"Auntie Gina, what are you bringing? Mama made gooseberry tarts . . ."

"And, oh, the sugar that took," Abbie mourned.

". . . and cinnamon rolls."

"Let me at 'em!" shouted Corky as he made a scramble toward the baskets and boxes.

"Corky, no!" By the time the rambunctious boy was settled down and the blankets rearranged, Abbie's world had righted itself, more or less.

"They're so excited about the party," she explained to Regina. "It's been a busy summer—but I hate to see it end."

Regina's gloved hand closed over Abbie's. "You're doing just fine—and you'll do just fine," she said gently.

"Let's say I'm doing better than I was at first," Abbie said ruefully, recalling her desperate appeals to Regina for help from time to time. "Now," she muttered, more to herself than to her friend, "if I can just make it through Christmas . . ." And when Regina squeezed her hand, Abbie thought she just might make it.

With determination, Abbie put aside the frightening aspects of her life and thought, with honesty, What more could a woman need? I have my man, my children, good friends, a beautiful night.

The wagon rattled over the frozen road, the stars cast their cold light, and the clouds drifted over a moon an arm's length away. And Abbie let drift away, for the moment, the weariness of the day's work, the niggling homesickness, the constant worry about being so far from a doctor, and, never completely forgotten, the isolation of the small house in the big bush.

This country! So beautiful, so terrible, so breathtaking, so heart-stopping. Was it possible to love it? Now, she acknowledged—as mercurial in her moods as the rain-spangled, star-drenched sky—she did well to endure it.

While Worth and Sam went to tie the horses to the fence and blanket them, Abbie, Regina, and the children carted the boxes and baskets inside, to be greeted by the friends gathered there, hang their wraps on hooks, and join the group holding cold hands to the warmth of the big heater. Through the grate's openings the fire blazed cheerily, and the iron side in one spot glowed cherry red. Damp gloves were piling up below the heater, and the smell of wet wool mingled with the fragrance of coffee coming to a boil on the stove's flat top.

The desks and benches had been shoved around to provide makeshift play areas. Several crokinole boards were in place with eager children practicing their skill in shooting the discs for the center hole. Someone had brought the amazing "Seroco Reversible Game Board" and was the envy of every child there (and numerous adults). It revolved on its own special stand, and—one side or the other—offered choices of such games as Chicago, pyramid, bottle-and-pin pool, three-ring, Carroms, checkers, and backgammon. At each end of the teacher's desk, domino games were underway; a checkerboard turned conveniently on the organ stool.

"Caro! Hey, Caro!" a voice piped from the front corner of the room, and a gnarled hand beckoned insistently.

"It's the uncles!" Carolyn said, surprised.

"Well, what do you know! What a lovely treat for Harry and Hubert," Regina said. "I suppose dear Willie is responsible."

It hadn't been easy. But when Harry and Hubert heard that Willie was going to the game party, their wistful eyes had been more than he could stand, being Willie.

"Would you fellas like to go?" he had asked, and it was enough to precipitate an hour of argument between the brothers.

"I could make it," Hu had begun, "but Harry's older'n me. I don't know about him . . ."

"I bin traipsin' you around since you was born!" Harry growled. "You'll probably misbehave, crazy kid that you are, so I'll have to go along, whether I want to or not."

"What about clothes?" Willie asked practically, and he spent more time than he had to give in digging out wrinkled pants, ironing them, finding socks that matched, rubbing spots from coats, and even polishing shoes.

"Think you can get supper over early, fellas?" Willie asked and then waited patiently through another round of give-and-take. The "fellas" were in high form, obviously. The only thing they regretted was that they hadn't known earlier that they were going; the anticipation would have carried them along for days, even as the afterglow would linger for days in their otherwise colorless lives.

And when Willie arrived, his lanky frame dressed in his Sunday best, his thatch of thick black hair freshly shorn, and his gaunt cheeks nicked from a round with a razor, Harry and Hubert were ready to go.

It was Willie who banked their fire, adjusted the damper, blew out the lamp, and helped the elderly men to the rig. It was Willie who wrapped them well against the night's piercing cold. It was Willie who assisted them into the schoolhouse, removed their wraps, and found a place—in front of a checkerboard—to sit. Consequently, it was with some relief Willie heard Hu's call to Carolyn Morris and saw her begin to make her way across the crowded room.

"Willieeeeee." It was Dolly Trimble. "Somebody needs to shake this grate . . ."

Carolyn kissed the scanty-haired heads of "uncles" Harry and Hubert, brought them each a cup of cocoa, located Hubert's handkerchief when a drop trembled on the tip of his nose, and set the board up for them.

"Why don't you each play with someone else, for a change?" she suggested.

"Sshh. Get this board set up quick! Grandma Dunphy's got her eye on Harry here!"

"She has? Where? Where?" Harry's rheumy eyes lifted, and Hu hissed, "She's the one behind the hearin' horn. Do you want to spend your night bellowin' into it?"

Going for a cocoa refill, Carolyn's heart came up into her throat: The door opened, and Ruby Lille stepped inside, followed by her daughter Violet and—Micah. Carolyn couldn't remember having seen Micah Lille at any local gathering since she was a small child and he a teenage boy.

But of course, she thought, Violet would want to come to one of the few social gatherings of the year. At the age of 13, she couldn't come by herself, and Ruby's health had been poor; obviously they had prevailed on Micah to bring them.

Ruby, a comfortable, dark-complected woman, went to join friends. Violet, called "Tiger" Lille because of her vivid coloring and lithe build, turned on quick, light steps to a corner where other girls her age were giggling, casting coy glances toward an area where equally self-conscious boys were roughhousing and casting surreptitious glances toward the girls.

No two people could be so dissimilar in personality as Tiger and her brother, Carolyn thought, studying Micah as he leaned casually against a wall at the far side of the room. At that moment his eyes lifted.

With a roomful of people between them, Carolyn saw only the proud face of Micah Lille; with the racket of a dozen games swelling around her, she heard only the beating of her own heart in her ears as the deep-set black eyes looked into her own until it seemed they must see beyond the surface. Could eyes see hearts?

As though drawn, Carolyn took a quick step toward Micah Lille. One step, two—and the door of the schoolhouse burst open and a distraught figure stumbled into the room.

8

As one person the entire crowd turned toward the desperate face of the man swaying in the open door. Even the children sensed that something was terribly wrong and looked toward their parents for reassurance.

For a moment there was stunned silence. The man's face worked, but he seemed unable to speak; rain glistened on his lashes like tears.

"Jamie! What's wrong, man?" It was Willie Tucker who broke the grip of fear that had swept with the wintery draft into the room. Willie stepped forward and placed his hand on James Jameson's arm. "What is it?"

"Dora! It's Dora!" Jamie said hoarsely. "She's gone!"

"Jamie," Willie said gently, "she's been gone before. You can count on every man here; we'll find her—never fear."

"But it's never been like this before!" Jamie said desperately. "This time she's been gone eight hours, maybe more!"

The crowd pressed close around the neighbor who had, in his helplessness and fear, turned to them for help.

"When I went in at noon," Jamie continued, "she was gone. At first I didn't worry. Sometimes she takes these walks . . ."

They all knew about Dora's walks. As if in a private dream—or perhaps a nightmare—she would start out across the fields or down the roads, searching.

"By the middle of the afternoon I began to worry." There was no way to describe the fear that had finally prompted him to bank the fire, dress warmly, take the dog, and head out—or the heartbreak with which he had called her name into the cold and silent sky and secret bush. He searched until dark for the wife who, maddened by a grief too keen to bear, had turned from him three years ago and who lived as a stranger in his house.

"It's almost nine o'clock," Jamie said, with anxiety-filled eyes. "As far as I can tell, she didn't take a coat."

The circle stirred as though a giant hand moved among them. They all knew what it meant to be caught in freezing weather. Being without adequate protection was a frightening thought.

"Let's get organized." Willie's voice was brisk. "Don't worry, Jamie. Everything will be all right." He spoke with a conviction he could not feel, and everyone knew it and appreciated him for the effort.

"We'll search farm by farm," Willie continued, as the men moved forward and the women and children stepped back. "Each man will take the responsibility for his own place. We can't wait for daylight. There's a moon most of the time, fortunately.

"We'll make headquarters here at the school. Someone will have to stay." His eyes searched the group. Many of the women had small children, and they were even now bundling them into their wraps, packing their boxes, and preparing to leave for home. Regina, stalwart, kindly Regina, stepped forward. Willie found his answer in her eyes. "Regina will stay," he announced.

"And I'll stay with her," Abbie said, her heart going out to the stricken-faced man standing just inside the door.

"Caro, will you take the children with you? Worth can search our place, and I'll keep your mother company."

"Brother Victor . . ." Jamie raised imploring eyes to the minister.

"Yes, Jamie, we'll pray." And there in the hush of the moment a silent cry went up from half a hundred hearts as the preacher led them in a simple petition.

When the last rig had departed, Regina closed the door and joined Abbie by the heater, shivering and holding out her hands to the warmth. "I'm afraid—terribly afraid," she said. "That rain is turning to ice almost as soon as it hits. And Dora—well, Dora isn't all that responsible."

How quickly the threat of the bush and the northern weather had challenged the brief respite of summer, turning lighthearted fun to gripping fear! Abbie was stunned by the suddenness of it all.

The women poured themselves cups of coffee and sat down, leaning elbows on the desks in front of them. They could almost feel the sting of the ice slashing through the black night, silvering into beauty on the lighted windowpanes. Regina began to tell Abbie the story only hinted at previously.

"It all happened about three years ago. It was terrible, one of the tragedies of the bush. Farm life isn't easy on women—you know that—and frontier life may be hardest of all.

"Crops were not good that year. If you didn't have any money, and most folks didn't, you were in a bad way. Several of the men went to Prince Albert to work in the gristmill; many went north to the woods. A few went as far as the coast."

Abbie nodded. The crop, she knew, was everything. When it failed there was little or nothing to fall back on. Newcomers, with no backlog, were particularly vulnerable.

"Jamie had no choice. We all know that," Regina said with a sigh. "And Dora knew it, or should have. But she was afraid—and who among us can blame her?—and refused to face facts and the need for Jamie's being away. The point of the whole thing is that she was called on to muster up a strength she just didn't have." Silently the women thought of the insurmountable problems facing a wife and mother with small children in her care, in the bush—in winter—alone.

"Jamie left his team with us so Dora wouldn't have the care of the horses," Regina continued. "We knew she didn't have any way to go anywhere, so Sam stopped by her place once in a while to check on her and the two boys. And, of course, Collum went every so often to clean the barn. The last time Sam was there the children were complaining of sore throats, but otherwise things were as usual. He chopped some wood for Dora, emptied the ashes for her, did a few things like that." Abbie, knowing Samuel Morris by now as a fine man and good neighbor, could visualize him being helpful to the lone woman.

Regina refilled the coffee cups and resumed her story. "One day I realized I hadn't see the boys going by to school all week. The more I thought about it the uneasier I got. Sam hitched the horse to a cutter, and I drove over. We don't do a lot of visiting here in the winter but—well, as I said, I was uneasy."

Regina had packed a box of goodies, wrapped herself up warmly, climbed into the cutter, and with harness and runners creaking sharply on the biting air, jolted and skidded over frozen snow-rutted roads toward the Jameson place. The day was brilliantly beautiful, all blue sky and white world. The horse's breath rose in fairy clouds and streamed behind the flying rig. Regina thoroughly enjoyed the outing—until she reached the Jameson place.

The driveway to the house was one smooth, unbroken drift of snow; it was clear that no one had been in or out recently. Regina felt a stir of alarm at the stillness of the scene. The Christmas-card setting was absolute; there was no sound or movement. A sense of something wrong nagged at the edges of thought.

And then she knew what it was: there was no smoke. No smoke from the stovepipe of the heater in the front room was not surprising; Dora had probably closed off that room and she and the boys were living, primarily, in the kitchen. But there was no smoke from the kitchen's stovepipe, and that was ominous.

Could Dora and the children be gone? She knew they could not; the unbroken snow gave plain evidence of that.

Regina slapped the reins on the horse's back, and the horse struggled through the unblemished expanse to the house. There were no tracks in the snow drifting across the porch; there was no answer to her knock.

Opening the door, she called. Her words seemed to linger in eery puffs of frozen breath. The frigidness of the room exceeded that of the great outdoors, where the bright sun at least played weakly on upturned faces.

"Dorrie!" she called, stepping inside. "Are you here?"

She crossed the linoleum, so rigid that it crackled underfoot, and entered the room beyond the kitchen. It, too, was empty and silent, the windows thickly frosted.

She eyed the stairs. Again she called, her voice ringing up the stairwell. Something impelled her up the steps, but a sickness rose in her throat as she went, a reluctance to proceed, and a fear born of the silence.

Pushing open one door she found the room empty. Entering the other room, her eyes flew to the bed. Three motionless ridges were humped side by side, two of them small, and in the middle, a longer one.

Regina approached the bed and saw, from the dim light seeping through the frost-encrusted panes, the tops of two small dark heads, and between them the staring, mad eyes of the woman.

Regina's voice broke, and she and Abbie sat in silence, reviewing the horror of that moment. The wind sweeping around the building added sound effects to Regina's story that were all too real.

"I dropped the coverlet over Dora's face—like she had it," Regina continued simply, "and got out of there somehow, and down the stairs. My mind seemed to be in shock, and my body moved automatically, doing what had to be done.

"I floundered through the drifts to the woodpile," she said, shivering. "Fortunately the axe had been left in the chopping block. I hacked away until I had some kindling, got myself back inside and built fires, first in the kitchen range and then in the heater in the other room. The house was incredibly cold. The rocks by the range I stuffed into the oven, and I pulled the teakettle to the front lids. It was full of ice, of course. Then I went back upstairs."

With force, Regina had pulled the covers from Dora's grip to find the boys dead. Looking at the small, lifeless forms and the almost equally rigid body of the mother, Regina had been overwhelmed with a feeling of impotence. When she could manage to speak, she had said, "Dorrie, listen to me. Can you hear me?" Her voice, raised to repeat the question, echoed in the stillness of the room. "'Dorrie, I've got to go for help. I'll have to leave you for a little while. I'm going for Sam. But I'll be back just as soon as I can.' I thought," she said to Abbie, "for one grisly moment of telling her to stay where she was . . . that it would soon be warm. I guess I was sort of hysterical by that time."

"I guess!" Abbie repeated.

"There was no flicker on Dora's face or in her eyes to indicate she heard—or cared," Regina continued, recounting how she had stumbled downstairs, checked the fires, added wood, adjusted the drafts, and hurried outside, closing the door on a scene more dreadful than she could have imagined.

"I careened into our yard like a mad woman myself, I guess," Regina said, "and Sam hurried to meet me. I babbled out the story, and he seemed to understand. He began to gather up things to take back with us, and he sent Collum on horseback to get Willie Tucker. Willie's a bachelor, you know, without family to expose to diphtheria, if that's what it was, and Sam suspected it right away. And we went back."

Sam, she said, had moved the two small bodies to the other bedroom, and she had brought up the warm rocks and packed them around the woman and rubbed her legs, arms, and body. Only with effort and patience could she force a little soup between Dora's lips.

"She didn't seem to be sick, then or later," Regina recalled. "It was strange. I think she just went out of her head, either when the boys were sick or when they died. I shudder to think how she placed them in that bed, made a place for herself in the middle, and climbed in with them. A sort of nest it was, and I think she would have died right there if I hadn't happened along." With a twisted smile Regina offered, "Spoiled her plans, I did.

"She could have gone for help, you know. We're not that far away. But no, she was going to go with the boys. That's why I'm so frightened for her tonight. She has no sense of survival. Well," Regina continued, "Willie arrived, as he always does in emergencies, and went about taking care of the little bodies. He and Sam made coffins. The boys were put in them and taken to the granary and placed side by side on sawhorses to await their father's arrival.

"I stayed with Dora until Jamie got home and the funeral was over. Brother Victor led a small procession to the cemetery—just a few friends and neighbors; no one feared contamination with everything so frozen, including the poor little bodies.

"Eventually Dora got up, even said a few words from time to time, although she never makes much sense. Mostly she's just silent."

"And Jamie?" Abbie questioned. Jamie was even now searching for the woman who probably didn't care, or even know, that she was lost.

"Poor Jamie. He's had his work cut out for him. His work and hers too. Sometimes I wonder who to feel the most sorry for." Regina's round face was filled with sympathy. "She, at least, lives in a world where hurts are shut out; Jamie is never free of pain. You see, he can't seem to forgive himself. He feels so guilty about what happened. He's tried hard to make it up to her, but it's no use. The truth of the matter is that while she lost her sons, he lost his sons and his wife."

The sad sound of the wind was dirgelike around the small building and the women sitting there. Heaven alone knew what it was doing to those out searching.

* * *

Jamie bent his head into the wind that was only slightly colder than his heart, and wiped away the moisture—half snow, half rain—that ran like tears down his face. Out here, alone, he faced not only his guilt but his hopelessness and his despair, and the trickling moisture was salty on his lips. Calling his wife's name into the night, he thought bitterly that he had really lost her three years ago.

When word of his sons' deaths had reached him, he had come home. What he had faced—the loss of his children and the withdrawal of his wife—had plunged his heart like a stone to the bottom of his being, where it had lain ever since. At times the beauty of the great Saskatchewan sky and the peace of the quiet earth had brought a measure of balm to his spirit. But when he opened the door to his house and faced the shuttered eyes of his wife, the weight returned.

At first he had tried to bridge the gap, to reach her and to let her know he shared her sorrow and grief. It was all too late. She would not, or could not, hear him. Only occasionally was there a slipping of the expressionless mask she wore, but the alternative was so dreadful it made the other seem a relief. For who can look on baleful eyes and a grimace of hate, unshaken?

There were times Jamie wished he could join her in her cocoon, insulated against the hurt. But he paid his debt the only way he knew, by caring for her as tenderly as he could. She—his wife—was his child now.

"Dorrie-e-e, Dorrie-e-e-e . . ." Her name, called into the wintry wind, slipped away in silence, even as she had.

*   *   *

It was Willie Tucker who found her. After searching his farm, his thoughts had turned to the river. That Dora would have had the strength to make it so far seemed incredible, but it should be searched. None of the Riverbank people—often transients—had been at the party; no one, insofar as Willie knew, would search that bush-bordered waterway. With a fresh supply of kerosene in his lantern, Willie headed for the river.

Here, the Saskatchewan ran well below the surface of the land, between deep trenches. The water, so soon to be the greenish-white of solid ice, was as low as it would be until the ice melted in the spring. In the dark, you could push through the high bushy escarpments and fall abruptly to the exposed rocks and sand below.

When the lantern light picked out the ragged shadows of broken grass and scuffed sand on the lip of the bank, Willie dropped to his knees and then to his stomach and wriggled his way to the edge, to swing the lantern at the end of his long arm into the void.

As the yellow arc touched the edge of the river, he saw the shadow lumped there. Knowing he had found her, he slid over the bank and to the water's edge. On the shingle she lay crumpled, shoeless, scratched, and wet.

With compassion, Willie pulled her back from the slapping, lapping waters and turned her so that the light fell on her cold face and set eyes. For a moment he huddled by her, his heart moved for her and the unfinished, final journey she had begun, and for Jamie, whose lonely journey would go on. Loneliness was something Willie knew about, although it would have astonished the district of Wildrose to hear it.

Finally Willie made his way along the shingle until he found a spot he could climb. From there it was a matter of 15 or 20 minutes until he woke the sleeping household of the nearest cabin.

When the stars had faded, and hope with them, he brought the jolting wagon—a rude catafalque—down the empty road toward the circle of men who waited, massed quietly around one of their number, his eyes tearless now in a caricature of a face as he stepped forward to claim his own.

Dora Jameson was buried between the graves of her two small sons. Only Regina Morris saw the significance of the long mound of fresh-turned earth, already freezing into a hardened shell, between the smaller ones on each side.

The frozen landscape was death personified. It was hard to keep one's heart fixed on the thought that a springtime would come, sweet grasses flourish and blow in mild winds, birds sing their glorious songs, and flowers fill the air with fragrance once again.

In Jamie's frozen face was no hope at all. Turning from the scarred earth, Regina placed her hand gently on the arm of her neighbor. "Jamie," she urged, "try not to spend useless time in grieving. Surely Dorrie's happy now. I think she's finally at rest. And—she's with the boys."

Jamie, recalling those twisting fingers, the mad stare, and the way Dora had gone on a restless search for only God knew what, agreed. He left the supportive circle of friends for the lonely routine of his life and found it no lonelier than he had remembered.

But occasionally he looked for eyes that held no softening glance and listened for a voice that held no warmth —and missed them. The shining light, for Jamie, had flickered and quenched a long time ago. That it would ever shine again he couldn't suppose.

9

I'm not making this trip again until it snows and we can go in the cutter!" The pronouncement came from Regina's tight lips in a chatter from the excessive bouncing and jolting of the buggy. The road, though snowless, was frozen in ridges and lumps from previous traffic, and the light rig jounced its occupants unmercifully. "Slow down, for mercy's sake!" Regina clutched the arm rest, and her generous figure rocked and rolled until the blanket threatened to slip from her knees.

Carolyn tightened the reins, and the horse slowed from a fast trot to a sedate walk. Carolyn's laughter, light and joyous, ringed her jaunty blue tam like a cloud. Regina eyed her daughter speculatively. If she didn't know better, she'd say the child was in love.

Carolyn, at 16, with her fragile body and delicate face, blue-veined white skin, light gray eyes, and quiet ways, had always elicited the tenderest responses from all who knew her; adults and children alike treated her as though she were a child who needed protection. Because of her sensitive nature and physical limitations, her parents worried over her, particularly now as she approached womanhood. With hearts yearning for her happiness and protection, they prayed for someone to come along for her, someone—perhaps an older man—who would protect and care for her as they did.

But such a one had not been forthcoming. Regina abandoned her suspicions and relaxed, in an effort to accept this "new" daughter. For Carolyn—until now an unformed creature, wrapped in a protective and restrictive cocoon—threatened to emerge as a creature of strength and dignity.

But only Carolyn herself recognized the thread of steel at the core of her being—never needed and so never revealed—that was vibrating under stimuli never encountered before. The sound, uncertain now, like the first tuning of a musical instrument, promised the sweetest and wildest of music.

Carolyn laughed again and loosed the reins, reveling in the cheek-tingling wind that whipped tendrils of fair hair from under the tam to stream behind in a most undignified manner.

"Hold on, Mum!" she sang, and Regina closed her eyes and hung on.

In Meridian, limping only slightly, Carolyn tied the horse loosely to the porch rail while Regina, fumbling with her own hair, entered the store, produced her list, and began assembling her supplies.

Carolyn pulled off her gloves and held her hands out to the warmth of the great heater in the center of the room. Her eyes were ashine, and her cheeks, usually pale, were glowing with color. But the color faded and her breath caught in her throat when a man turned from the window of the small post office in the corner of the room, and her eyes met those of Micah Lille.

Micah stood where he had turned, studying Carolyn with intense eyes. Deliberately those eyes turned to sweep around the store, resting briefly on Regina at the counter in the rear. Then, with quick, lithe steps, Micah moved to Carolyn's side.

The intensity of that gaze, now only inches above her, silenced the greeting trembling on her lips, and ran like warm syrup throughout her body. Her knees weakened, and she almost staggered with the force of that visual contact.

The man's sculptured lips softened slightly, and he spoke, tautly, meaningfully: "I'm cutting wood at the lake." And then he was gone.

On the ride home, their purchases bulked around them, Regina relaying to her daughter various bits of news garnered in her brief time in the store, Carolyn's silence went unnoticed.

"Oh, and I picked up Hubert's and Harry's mail," Regina said. "There's a small package for them . . . their catalog order, I guess. You can take it the next time you go."

"Tomorrow," Carolyn said. "I'll go tomorrow."

"But you just went yesterday," her mother objected.

"Tomorrow," Carolyn repeated. And the steel tightened and the sound it gave forth was no longer uncertain.

* * *

While Regina clucked and frowned, Carolyn prepared to take the Runyon brothers' package to them.

"Let Collum take it, if it's so important," Regina argued. "You were out yesterday, and you didn't look too well when we got home, either. I think it was too much for you."

"Tommyrot, Mum. Actually, it did me good. Today will do me good." Carolyn spoke with a confidence that made Regina shake her head.

"Well, take this loaf of bread to Hubert and Harry," Regina said resignedly. "Would you like me to come along?" she asked suddenly.

"There's no need, Mum," Carolyn said in a somewhat smothered voice. "I'm sure I'll be just fine."

Regina followed her daughter to the porch and stood, arms wrapped in her apron, while Carolyn climbed up into the buggy, placing the bread and the mail-order package at her feet, arranging a blanket over her knees. With a wave and a smile, she rattled away.

Out of her mother's sight, the casual smile faded, color heightened her thin cheeks, and her eyes glittered. The night had been spent in tossing and turning, dreaming—both in and out of sleep—of the magnetic eyes and tempting mouth of the man called Micah Lille. They drew her today with a sort of hypnotism. Almost, she thought, she would have climbed over her mother's body, so single-minded was her purpose.

Turning off on the lakeshore road, Carolyn was soon on Lille land. Before she saw him through the leafless trees and bushes, she heard the ring of his axe.

Carolyn pulled into the small clearing and stopped the horse. In spite of the cold, Micah had laid his coat aside, and the muscles rippled under the dampness of his shirt as he swung the axe against the bole of a black poplar. Seeing her at last, he laid the axe down, picked up his coat, flung it over his shoulder, and strode to the buggy.

Leaning against the buggy wheel, he looked at Carolyn for a long moment. Then, "Get down," he said abruptly, and she did.

Face-to-face with him, and alone, Carolyn stilled the trembling in her limbs and raised her chin and looked as steadily into his eyes as he did into hers.

With a muttered exclamation, Micah reached for her, pulled her fiercely against him and bent his head, all in one swift motion.

His lips, when they met hers, did so harshly, even cruelly. Finally, lifting his head, he stared down at her, his dark eyes burning. Carolyn met his gaze steadily, unaware that though her cheeks had paled, her eyes were as unflinching as his. Her lips, pulsing from the pressure of his, were still lifted, waiting.

With what sounded very much like a groan, Micah thrust her from him. "What's the matter with you!" he gritted. "Don't you know nice girls don't do that!"

"It seemed very—nice to me."

This time it was a definite groan. "Why have you looked at me as you have, at the social—in the store?"

Carolyn didn't pretend ignorance. "Why?" she asked. "What did you see in my look?"

"If I ever saw an invitation in a woman's eyes, there was one in yours," Micah said, heavily.

"And this troubles you."

"I'm flesh and blood, girl!"

"Yes, and very nice flesh and blood," Carolyn said softly, and Micah looked—first startled, then grim.

"And nice girls don't say things like that," he gritted.

Carolyn stepped forward until she leaned against him, and lifted her face to his. Micah's jaw tightened and he turned his head; his arms remained at his side.

Puzzlement filled Carolyn's eyes. Stepping back, she said, "Micah, I don't think you quite understand. I'm not playing 'nice' or 'naughty.' In fact, I'm not playing at all."

Micah, for one brief moment, seemed to stop breathing. Then, "Get back in the buggy," he said roughly, and quietly Carolyn did so.

Studying his set face, darker somehow than usual, Carolyn looked down from the buggy seat, not moving, waiting for his eyes to meet hers. "Look at me, Micah," she said softly.

Almost against his will, he looked. And he groaned. Snatching his jacket from the buggy wheel where he had laid it, he strode off.

Carolyn watched, a soft smile on her lips, while he flung down the jacket, picked up the axe, and sunk the blade with unnecessary force into the tree trunk.

Feeling stronger than she ever had in her life, Carolyn wheeled the rig out of the clearing. Wonderingly, she touched the tip of her finger to her burning mouth.

10

*T*he snowfall started in late afternoon, great, white flakes drifting down so lazily that they could hardly be suspected of harboring grim purposes. Nor did it seem possible that they could long survive (cupped in a mittened hand, the fragile wonders slowly faded away to nothingness), but Wildrose people knew better. Like stitches in a lengthening muffler, the dainty flakes would bond into a suffocating mass by morning.

Familiar paths to barn and well and woodpile were quickly obliterated; a carelessly dropped hammer or saw was lost for the duration of the long season; noxious manure piles, dingy coops, and heaped cordwood were disguised as pristine mountains.

Jamie Jameson trudged through a drifting curtain of snowflakes from the barn to the house. Shutting the door behind him, he lit the lamp, blew out the lantern, hung it by the door, and his empty world closed around him. Automatically he stirred the fire, added wood, pulled a pot of beans to the front of the range from the back lid where they had been simmering all day, and in a matter of moments had assembled the rest of his supper—a hunk of bread slathered with butter (still oozing buttermilk, he noted sourly), and a cup of reheated coffee. The popping of the woodfire was the only sound aside from the rattling of the stovepipe with an occasional gust of wind.

When it seemed he could stand the loneliness and the silence no longer, he pulled off his boots, wrapped himself in a quilt, and went to sleep on the bed he had moved downstairs after Dora's funeral for convenience and comfort, and in an effort to leave his cold, cold memories behind.

Though winter had barely begun, Jamie found himself longing for spring.

* * *

Uneasy under the evening's unnatural hush, glancing through the window at the ceaseless, pitiless inundation of snow, Abbie Rooney resisted a silly impulse to count heads: "One, two, three, four, all present and accounted for."

Like a mother hen she stretched anxious wings over her brood. The circle of light and warmth seemed so tiny under the big sky, and the house so small and hidden in the deep bush. With a near passion of solicitude she gathered her chicks about her, pulled her chair near Worth's, and shut out the lonely silence.

Spring and flowers and soft breezes and sunshine seemed a million days and a thousand dreams away.

* * *

Willie Tucker, to whom winter was just another season out of four, settled down by the fire after supper for a rare rest. With his thick-thatched head against the back of the rocker and his deep-set eyes shut in his gaunt face (people said Willie was the spittin' image of Abraham Lincoln), he considered the next day's tasks.

His own home, set in order years ago by his mother and faithfully maintained by Willie, required no immediate attention. Even now, damp socks dangled neatly from a wire stretched behind the range, and yeast worked in a crock for the next baking. His concern was, as always, for someone else—in this case the Runyon brothers and their helplessness.

Happy as larks with their new spectacles, Hubert and Harry would brighten considerably, though snowbound, if he shared with them the papers and other publications he had amassed. Having lived in the States, the brothers would relish the recent account of a Montana man who killed one of his chickens for dinner and found a quantity of gold nuggets in its crop and gizzard. Thirty-one chickens had scratched in the same patch, and the man at once began a "course of postmortem prospecting." Nuggets were found in each chicken, to the total value of over $300. The man invested in 50 chickens and turned them out to do "mine-scratching." After two days he killed one chicken and mined two dollars' worth of gold from its crop. This was considered, *The Youth's Companion* reported, the most successful chicken business ever attempted.

Just thinking about the unending discussion this news would generate between Hubert and Harry, Willie's craggy, rather lugubrious face broke into a smile.

Halfway through a story himself, Willie pulled the lamp close, adjusted the wick, and began to read where he had left off the previous night: *Donning the lovely gown of her mother's making, a thoughtless daughter hurried away, trying not to see the worn, weary face that told without words of the midnight hours spent in painful stitching. If the mother-sewed seams could repeat to the daughter who wore it the prayers, the fears, the dreams, stitched into them by the flying needle perhaps the mother who fashioned them would be made happier oftentimes by a word of appreciation.*

If Willie saw any similarity between the unthanked seamstress and himself, no one would ever suspect it. Life took from Willie Tucker more than it gave; that's the way it was. The good Lord kept Willie in the state of single blessedness, most people believed, just so he could fill in all the gaps and nooks and needs of the district. Thank-yous, for Willie, were no more necessary than to bless the sun for its warmth.

Tomorrow, Willie thought, if the roads were passable, he'd get over to Harry's and Hubert's, take the magazines, fresh milk, a few eggs, and replenish their water supply and fill their woodbox.

Even so, could the elderly men make it through another winter? Would there be another spring for Harry and Hubert?

* * *

In the Morris home, Carolyn pulled back the stiffly starched curtain and watched the falling snow despairingly. As the farmyard disappeared under a thickening blanket, so, she knew, did the clearing in the woods where Micah Lille was cutting a year's supply of firewood for his parents.

No matter that he had so strangely thrust her from him after so passionately kissing her. Whatever the reason—and Carolyn suspected Micah had some sort of misplaced idea that she couldn't possibly be interested in a man who was half Indian—she was confident that she was more than a match for his misgivings. Having found the one man in the world (well, her small world) whom she could love, Carolyn knew herself to be strong enough for whatever resistance she might face from Micah—or her parents.

She prowled the house from window to window until her mother said, "It's here to stay, honey. You'll see plenty of snow before spring."

Spring! Could she live until then without seeing Micah, or seeing him only briefly? Would he be content to stay in Wildrose, or would he go north, as before?

Like a mouse in a maze, Carolyn's mind skittered around, trying to come up with ways and means to be with Micah Lille. Spring, for Carolyn, had never seemed more cruelly remote.

*T*he bedraggled Christmas tree had finally been dis-
mantled and taken outside, where it leaned on the
woodpile, a splotch of green and a wisp of fragrance. Corcoran and Cameron, back in school after the holidays, had
grudgingly agreed to its removal.

The holiday season had gone better for Abbie than she
had dared hope, although she had a tearful moment when
the package from "back home" arrived and the tissue-
wrapped, mysterious gifts were placed under the tree
along with the meager ones she and Worth provided.

Christmas Day had been spent with the Morrises. Abbie had baked the buns and the pumpkin pies for the dinner held at midday; everything, it seemed, rotated around
chore time.

Although Abbie had considered getting into the shed
and locating a "Demi-Plume" of ostrich feathers she knew
was in there somewhere ("We do not handle the poor,
fluffy goods," the Ontario merchant had declared prideful-
ly), envisioning how it would brighten Regina's obviously
ancient black velvetta hat, good sense had prevailed. Regina would continue to wear her featherless hat, but her
kitchen now boasted a set of hot pads. Handstitched by
Abbie during long, dark evenings, the task had fixed her

attention on something—anything—other than the winter wind sweeping around the isolated cabin, rattling the flimsy stovepipe, piling against the windows. Regina had given Abbie an apron fashioned from a scrap of corded dimity left over from Caro's summer dress, and featherstitched, to be both useful and pretty.

Now, wearing the apron and sweeping up the pine needles with Merry importantly helping, Abbie realized she had come through the season satisfactorily, and a soundless "So there!" was directed triumphantly toward the bush that so tended to intimidate her. Sometimes she fancied it crouched just an arm's length away, waiting for—she knew not what. Ontario and the gentle life seemed, at these times, far, far away, and loneliness, like summer's sandhill fleas, chewed at her painfully.

"I'll make it yet, or die trying!" she muttered grimly, flinging the pine needles into the heater. The scent of all outdoors filled the house and Abbie sighed, caught once more between the beauty and the threat of the bush.

Suddenly the house seemed too small. Impulsively, Abbie threw off her apron. "Merry," she said, "how would you like to get out for a while?"

"O-ooh, yes!" Merry said, her blue eyes brightening as she struggled with the ties of her pinny.

Though the day was intermittently sunny, the weather was exceptionally cold. Abbie bundled her small daughter in several layers of clothing, with a final wrap of woolly scarf twined around her neck between knitted toque and coat collar. Merry peered drolly out, looking for all the world like the overstuffed baby doll her grandmother had sent her for Christmas. Abbie kissed the tip of the chapped nose lovingly and put on her own wraps and three-buckle, gum-rubber gaiters.

"We'll leave a note for the boys," she said, "just in case they get home before we do." She rummaged for a scrap of paper and a pencil and scribbled a hasty note, propping it against the ruby pickle caster and tong set in the center of the round oak table.

"Where are we going, Mummy?" Merry asked in muffled tones, tipping her head back in order to see her mother's face through the small slit between scarf and toque.

"To find Daddy," Abbie decided on the spot. After all, where else *could* they go? And the trail to the back part of the section would be comparatively easy to walk since Worth and the horse and stoneboat had been over it numerous times in the past few days.

"Can I ride on the stoneboat, Mummy?"

"Most likely, if Daddy's ready to come home." Abbie checked the damper, pulled on her fleece-lined kid mittens, and opened the door.

Worth was felling trees for the never-ending need of fuel. With luck he could haul them in before they were hidden under a fresh fall of snow, but wherever they lay, they could weather for next season's supply.

Restless at the winter's enforced inactivity, Worth was working alone at the muscle-stretching, blood-tingling job, obviously enjoying the physical effort required. Eventually, with help, the trees would be sawed into cordwood and stacked near the house.

Abbie and Merry crossed the yard and entered the bush, following the track left by the dragging stoneboat, a wide, low sled made of two peeled logs and crossboards. A few light flakes of snow blew onto their clothing where they clung, starlike, against the dark material. An occasional *plop* announced the falling of snow from an overburdened branch. Abbie pointed out the ever-present chickadees, thinking with amusement that they were just smaller versions of the happy, bouncing bundle at her side.

"There's Beauty," Merry cried when at last they caught a glimpse of the horse, a brushstroke of rust on a colorless palette.

The rangy animal, certainly no beauty, stood patiently on three feet, resting the fourth, its head lowered. Merry trotted ahead, eager to surprise her father.

"Daddy!" she called, adding in a disappointed voice when her mother pulled alongside, "Where's Daddy? I don't see him!"

"Where in the world could he be?" Abbie's eyes studied the surrounding bush, and she listened for the sound of the axe—or Worth's distinctive whistle.

"Worth?" she called. "Worth?" There was only the sighing of the wind through bare branches, and the skirmishing of loose snow over hardened drifts. A sound like that of a muffled drum broke the silence, and Abbie realized it was her own heartbeat pounding in her ears under the close-fitting band of her knitted cap.

It was odd that Worth would leave the horse huddled in the cold while he went off somewhere. And where could he go? There were no betraying tracks. Abbie tensed as she searched the small clearing with its toppled trees, lopped branches, and ragged stumps.

Merry and Abbie stepped into the virgin drift of snow alongside the stoneboat and ploughed their way around the sled to the horse. Merry raised a mittened hand to Beauty's frost-specked nose and laughed as the loose lips nibbled the wool; the sound pierced the air like an icicle in flight.

Abbie's eyes roamed the bush with a growing sense of foreboding. Suddenly it seemed as if a giant hand squeezed the breath from her body. Beyond the fallen trees and fresh-cut stumps lay a quiet lump, dark against the snow. For dreadful seconds she was as frozen and lifeless as the rigid tree trunks around her. The drum increased the tempo of its beat.

Swiftly she stepped in front of Merry and turned her around, toward home, saying, in a voice that meant no arguing allowed, "I want you to go home, Merry. I'll follow soon. Just stay in the tracks. Don't dawdle and don't play." The child raised big eyes, the scarf around her face thick with icy droplets where her breath had frozen in the wool.

"The boys will be there," Abbie added. "Tell them I'll be there soon. Go now. Show Mummy what a big girl you are."

Abbie watched until the dumpy figure struggled around the stoneboat and began its plod homeward. Then, numb with apprehension, she stumbled to the motionless man. Calling his name, she dropped to her knees at his side.

Except for the color of his face, as bleached as the snow which cradled it, Worth might have been asleep, face pressed into the pillow. He should have wakened when her hand touched his shoulder. But he did not. He did not!

Fearfully Abbie pulled him over. As she turned him, his unseeing eyes as empty as the sky into which they stared, a small crimson circle in the snow was revealed. Abbie leaned toward it and stared down into the small opening, no larger than Worth's pocket watch; red-rimmed it was, a lascivious mouth opening to a scarlet throat. Her hands flew to the collar of Worth's jacket. As it fell open, she saw with horror the hole gaping raggedly in his neck.

He lay in the embrace of the tree that took his life. As it had fallen, it had twisted unexpectedly toward him— locked in immobility by knee-deep snow—and a brittle limb had snapped as it came. The broken point, as sharp as a Chipewyan spear, plunged into the vulnerable spot between firm chin and sturdy shoulder, piercing the jugular vein. Impaled, he fell with the tree, to be released at the last to lie, stunned, as his life had run, swiftly and hotly, into the snow pressed against the terrible wound.

A small keening sound escaped Abbie's lips, equaling in eeriness the wind that sifted fresh snow over the chiseled face of her husband. The stamp of the horse's foot startled her and brought coherent thought.

To drag Worth's bulkily clothed body to the stoneboat and lift him to it, low though it was, was an impossibility—Abbie's cold hands slipped helplessly over the wool of his coat. And she refused to pull him by a leg; Worth should be treated, in death, with the dignity that had marked his life.

She rolled the body back to its original position; a warm compassion refused to leave Worth staring, sightless, into vast emptiness.

In a more rational moment Abbie would have realized the absurdity of what she was about to do, but at the time she was incapable of leaving Worth alone. Making her way to the animal, she grasped the bridle. Beauty, startled from her somnolence, jerked her head, almost lifting Abbie from her feet. Urging the horse forward, Abbie led her until she stood—head down, reins dragging—alongside the master who would not unhitch her that night or ever rub her down or feed her again. Abbie was strangely comforted at the arrangement.

* * *

When Abbie reached the house, pushed open the door, and stumbled in, her face a mask of snow and frozen tears, the twins were in the process of buttering bread. Their happy welcome was silenced at the sight of their mother's face.

"Daddy's hurt," Abbie managed, in response to their torrent of questions. "You'll have to go to Uncle Sam for help." They were soon bundled into their warm clothing, bread forgotten, stumbling over snow-rutted roads for the neighbor.

Merry crept into her mother's arms and Abbie held her close and rocked silently until she heard the creak of sleigh runners. Samuel Morris flung open the door and burst in, followed by Regina and the twins.

"Abbie?" Sam's voice was anxious as his eyes sought those of the woman sitting in the gloom.

Abbie raised empty eyes to his disturbed and questioning gaze. "It's Worth, Sam."

"What in heaven's name has happened!"

"It was the bush—the bush—"

*   *   *

When the sad night's work was done and Abbie was left—alone at her insistence—with her loved one, Sam went home, where Regina waited in the warm kitchen and the Rooney children were asleep upstairs. They talked about Abbie's words.

"She's had a fear of the bush all along," Regina said. "I think it typifies loneliness for her—separation from her family."

"It's as if she feels it took Worth from her," Sam said, reaching for a cup of coffee. "And in a way it did."

"It seems to me you either love the bush or hate it," Regina said thoughtfully, adding with a surprised note when there was no response from Sam and he avoided her look, his eyes studying his cup, "Sam! Don't tell me you wonder—after all this time—about me!"

Sam's face was a little sheepish. "Well," he said, "all this just sort of raised a question in my mind. After all, you're a long, long way from home—"

"This is home, Sam. This is home."

*   *   *

Worth was buried in the bleak Meridian cemetery in a grave hacked out by pickaxe on a day so dreary there seemed no chance of a spring ever again.

As if resentful of the wound in the bosom of the earth and the soiling of her robe, a bitter storm bent upon the mourners as they turned homeward. The roadways were all but obliterated. Horses plodded by instinct to remembered barns while drivers huddled on sleigh seats, blinded by the stinging snow, and their families crouched below in a thick bed of straw, covered with heavy quilts.

Reaching home, they struggled inside, poking up the coals and opening drafts until stoves glowed red-hot. With each blast of wind a drift of white sifted under the doors until rugs were thrust tight against them. Smoke was swept away as soon as it lifted from the lip of the tin stovepipes that trembled above snow-packed roofs.

"Are you sure you won't change your mind and come home with us?" Regina had asked Abbie anxiously as they prepared to leave the cemetery.

"Thanks, Regina," Abbie said, "but the children need to be home. We'd only have to go eventually." She helped Corcoran and Cameron and Merry into the Morris's sleigh and covered them.

"Have you had time to think about . . . what you'll do?"

"A little." Abbie climbed in and tucked the quilt around her.

"Will you go to Ontario?" Regina settled herself beside her friend.

Abbie hesitated, thinking of the black mound already whitening under a downy blanket. "I've written my folks, of course. I'm hoping my mother will come. I'll know more when I talk to her." And they huddled together under the storm's barrage.

In the half dark Sam and Regina deposited Abbie and the children at their door. Earlier Sam and Jamie Jameson, the other near neighbor, had cared for the wood and water and stock, even though Abbie had felt she could "manage."

Before Abbie could stop him, Sam alighted, went inside, lit the lamp, opened the stove, and chunked wood into it. "Abbie," he said, "you'll have to let us help." When she was silent, he added, "Jamie and I will be over in the morning to talk about it."

As he turned to go, Abbie put her hand on his arm, and her lips trembled as she said raggedly, "God bless you, Sam, you and Regina."

Sam's compassionate gaze spoke of his sympathy for the young woman's great sorrow and great need, and her effort at dignity in the face of them.

Abbie closed the door and stood with her back against it, feeling it vibrate with the force of the storm. Pitting her puny strength against it, she stood between it and her children. Only when Merry said, "I'm hungry, Mummy," did she fasten the latch against the battering force and draw a rug across the threshold.

12

*T*hough the wind had abated by morning, snow continued to fall. Abbie had no way of knowing whether or not school was open but opted to keep the twins home for the rest of the week, for her sake as much as theirs.

Jamie arrived early and did the milking, leaving quickly for home and his own chores. He returned in the afternoon, with Sam, and took a seat in the small front room; with grim looks they acknowledged the full water pail and the overflowing woodbox. Abbie's coat by the door was damp and her overshoes sat in a puddle of melted snow.

The children were painting quietly at the table as the three adults sat down to a cup of coffee by the heater.

"I don't know what your plans are," Sam said.

Abbie stared thoughtfully into her cup.

"I'm assuming, though, that you'll be pulling up stakes and going to Ontario," Sam continued. "But as long as you're here, I want you to know you can depend on my help." If he entertained a brief thought that his offer of help for Dora Jameson hadn't been enough, or if the others thought of it, it wasn't mentioned.

But Jamie's offer was made in urgent tones. "I'll help. You can count on me, Abbie." His fine dark eyes were sympathetic. In them one could read the memory of his own great loss and his concern for another woman—alone.

"Thank you both," Abbie said, "but I want to manage by myself as much as possible. I'm hoping to hear from my mother soon, saying she's coming, and then I can make my plans."

She glanced at the children. "We've talked, a little. The boys insist they can help, and I think they can." Her composure seemed to surprise the men, who appeared to be prepared for despair and hysteria, and certainly tears.

"If one of you will take the horses for now," Abbie asked, and Sam nodded agreement, "I'll keep the cow here; we'll need the milk and butter. And, of course, there's the calf." Abbie looked down at the slim hands in her lap, the hands that had never previously milked a cow except as a laughing experiment, and she remembered Sam's study of them when they first met. Well, she thought grimly, we shall see what they can do.

"Abbie," Jamie broke in strongly, "I'll do the milking. It's a walk of less than half a mile, shorter if the drifts are frozen in the fields and I can come that way."

Abbie's chin went up and her voice was firm when she said, "Thank you, Jamie, but it won't be necessary." Jamie, shaking his head, subsided.

"We'll come regularly, however," Sam interjected smoothly, "and do what we can—getting hay in from the stack, mucking out the barn . . ."

"I plan to do those things." The men's brows darkened and their mouths tightened, and Abbie smiled. "There can't be anything all that hard about pitching a little manure, can there?"

Sam and Jamie looked at each other helplessly. True, there were women who might manage farm chores, but obviously they didn't think Abbie Rooney was one of them.

Although it was a little early for evening chores, Sam and Jamie, as Abbie objected, headed for the barn before they went home.

"Pitch a little manure, indeed!" Jamie fumed as soon as the barn door closed behind them.

Sam shook his head unbelievingly as he stripped off his gloves and prepared to milk the cow.

Jamie took a pitchfork and speared hay furiously. "Have you ever seen such a proud one?"

"Not so much proud, Jamie," Sam said thoughtfully, "as independent."

"It's a fantasy she can't afford! Nor can she keep it up! Think of it, Sam—a woman, in the dead of winter, alone."

Sam glanced sharply at Jamie, but he was staring off into emptiness.

* * *

When Jamie Jameson and Sam Morris awoke the next morning and crawled out of warm covers to the frigid air of another bitter day, the thoughts of each went to the small, lonely log house, snow to the windowsills, where there was no man to build the fires.

It was not until Sam noted a thin wisp of smoke coming from the chimney across the field that he was able to breathe a sigh of relief and go about his work.

Jamie, not able to see the Rooney house because of the bush, made his way over snow-drifted fields until he, too, caught a glimpse of smoke—and was able to return to the chores of his day with a semblance of peace.

Abbie had wakened to the gray light of morning, the stone at her feet no colder than the one in her breast. She fought against waking, but the responsibilities of the day pressed in on her and a wave of misery swept over her. Gritting her teeth, she threw back the covers and flew to the heater. Grimly pleased to find she had stoked the stove well enough so that a few coals remained, she stuffed in kindling (and felt a small surge of pride that she had remembered it last night), blew on the embers until they blazed, added several pieces of dry wood, slammed the door, and scurried back to the warmth of the bed.

It wasn't a wise thing to do. The terrible loss she had suffered, the overwhelming responsibilities that were hers, the very loneliness of the bed—all swept over her with the force of a winter storm.

"Worth . . . ," she cried silently. But Worth wasn't there; he would never be there.

"God . . . ," she cried. And He was there. He would always be there.

When the worst of the chill was gone—from her heart as well as the house—Abbie took her clothes and returned to the fire to dress. That done, she went to the kitchen and lit the fire in the range.

The water in the bucket was frozen, but she had dipped water into a washbasin the night before (another small victory) and she put it on the stove to melt and heat for washing purposes. The water in the teakettle thawed quickly and boiled, and she made a pot of tea; with a cup of the steaming brew in her hand she returned to the heater and took a chair by the fire to think and plan before her day grew riotous with children and their demands and needs.

Chores were her chief concern; she must do them before the boys went to school so that she could leave Merry in the house with them. Isolation could be traumatic for an adult; for a child it could be disastrous. And there was always the threat of fire.

The immediate problems of her day—forcing Abbie to rational thought, demanding all her attention—were healing, in their way. Grief was crowded to the back of her heart. Common sense held her steady and got her on her feet, into the kitchen to fill a pot with water and reach for the rolled oats.

While the porridge was bubbling, Abbie set the table. Going into the small bedroom, she wakened the children as cheerily as she could. They brought their clothes to the heater, their day beginning with the routine they had always known, and Abbie prepared to go to the barn.

"When you've got your clothes on," she said, "sit up to the table and eat your breakfast." She doled out porridge, set out brown sugar and milk, and took thawed bread from the warming oven.

Corcoran grabbed a sock from Cameron and a tussle ensued, and Merry laughed. Abbie called, "Did you hear me?"

The children's united "Yeah" and prompt return to their scuffle relieved Abbie by its very normalcy and helped her through the door. Nevertheless, before she closed it she warned, "Don't touch the stoves!"

She hadn't gone 10 feet from the step before she made up her mind to wear a pair of Worth's trousers in the future, for the wind blew cruelly around her legs, and the snow that had drifted over the path in the night sifted into the tops of her overshoes. And when she perched on the milking stool, her skirts were in the way as she tried to clutch the pail with her knees. Maybe it sits on the floor, she thought, wishing she had paid more attention.

Within minutes her hands ached from the unaccustomed effort, and the cow, aware of her inept fumbling, moved impatiently. "Whoa, Cinderella!" she said firmly, feeling a little foolish and wondering why in the world they couldn't call their cow Bossy or Daisy like everyone else.

When she could no longer force her cramped hands to work, she loosed Prince Charming (what else!), who spraddled his front legs alongside his mother, bunted her masterfully with his small head, and began to suck, his tail working as happily as his jaws.

Setting the pail carefully by the door, Abbie took the pitchfork and tossed hay into the manger; Cinderella dropped her head docilely into the sweet fragrance. "Maybe if I do that first," Abbie mused, "milking would go better."

It was with a small feeling of accomplishment she patted the cow's warm rump, picked up the pail, opened the barn door, and started for the house.

Once inside, Abbie realized she was hungry. She scraped the porridge pot, filled a small bowl with the gooey substance, added fresh milk and brown sugar, and stirred it to gruel consistency, golden in color. While another pot of tea steeped, she picked up her breakfast and went to join the children in the other room. The usually despised oatmeal seemed tastier than she had remembered, and she could understand how Worth had come in from chores to enjoy a huge bowlful while she had shuddered and nibbled toast and jam. Her throat thickened and tears smarted behind her eyelids.

The people of Wildrose, shocked by the tragedy, reeled with the pain felt by one of its own. In their own way they did what they could. Friends dropped by when the weather permitted to offer solace and comfort and to leave fresh baked goods or the best cuts of newly butchered meat. No one went to Meridian without stopping to ask if they could get something from the store for her, and they returned with her mail. Sam and Jamie came regularly, and Brother Victor, often with his wife in tow, brought the wisdom of practical counsel and the healing of prayer.

And one day the letter she was awaiting was handed to her. Her mother was coming. Abbie put her head on the table and wept. Hot tears splashed on the shiny oilcloth and puddled there, to freeze during the night into a chip of ice.

13

*T*he bright sun silvered blindingly on frosted branches, snowcapped fence posts, and open fields of hard-packed drifts. Driving the cutter through a world of gems, Carolyn was unresponsive to the beauty, the expression on her face was disconsolate. The mare required no attention—to have strayed from the track was well-nigh impossible—and Carolyn gave herself to her dismal thoughts.

Weeks had passed with no contact with Micah Lille. That he remained in Wildrose she knew from conversation, at meeting time, with Ruby and Tiger, his mother and sister.

Church, she thought uneasily, was not a place one would expect to find Micah Lille, and a pang of guilt touched Carolyn, a church-raised girl—but only momentarily. With her new self-confidence, and with the blitheness of youth, she reasoned that Micah would be influenced toward spiritual values through her.

But when? Normally a patient person, Carolyn was experiencing a tumult of impatience, driven by a force she hadn't known before and didn't fully understand. But she called it love.

To the tune of creaking runners and jingling harness, Carolyn covered the road from home to the Runyon place.

From a slight elevation she could see over the bush to the lake and the rink that was kept cleared each winter by the youth of the district. Three homesteads touched on the lake; the Lille place was one of them. Now she could see a lazy lift of smoke from the log house at the lake's edge. She wondered if the sturdy building held the muscular body of Micah Lille, with its coiled-spring look of strength.

A movement between the shoreline and the rink caught her eye; a dark-clothed figure against the white background drew her attention. Micah Lille was cutting ice.

She knew what she would do.

* * *

"Just keep movin', Harry," Hubert said to his brother as Harry shuffled across the snowy porch, a bucket in his hand. "When you stop, I'll know you're dead."

"Or froze," Harry sniffed, his breath ringing his head and his long nose turning red. Getting his balance, he tipped the pail over the edge of the porch. "Too bad we ain't got no pigs to eat this slop," he said regretfully, as potato peelings, bacon rinds, eggshells, and table scrapings bonded almost immediately with the discards tossed there previously.

Tottering back to the half-open door, he handed the empty pail to Hubert. "Now give me the ashes," he ordered. Making his careful way to the other end of the porch, he dumped the contents of the pail over the edge. Wisps of ash whirled away, widening the unsightly mound. Praying for fresh snow was a simpler matter, the brothers had grimly decided, than hauling the ashes farther away.

When the brothers had shut the door on the crisp, clear air, even their fading senses caught the disagreeable odors of old men in confined quarters improperly cared for and, momentarily, their humor failed them.

"Face it, Hu," Harry said when they had gained the sanctuary of their comfortable, disreputable chairs beside the heater, "we ain't as young as we used to be."

"Hey, speak for yourself! If I remember correctly, you're older'n me, Harry. Or have you been lying to me all these years?"

"You're losin' your memory too, Hu."

Hubert sobered. "My memories are good enough," he said, and both men nodded scanty-haired heads in agreement.

Harry shook himself from reverie and glanced at the ancient desk in the corner of the room. Hubert, reading his mind, lifted himself from the chair and went to it. "Bein's as how I'm the youngest, and definitely the spryest, I'll get it."

Hubert pulled an envelope from the clutter and returned to the fireside. He held it out toward his brother.

"Read it, Hu. I want to hear it again."

"But you've already got your specs on."

"Yours are on your head, Hu."

With a chagrined grimace Hubert pulled his spectacles into place, peered at his brother, and said, "Now I know why I keep 'em up there—you're so all-fired ugly through them. You look like the last potato from the bottom of the barrel, all wrinkled and hairy."

"And you look just like me, everyone says. Now read the letter."

"It says, 'Dear brothers-in-law.' But that ain't right, Harry."

"I know that, Hu. I got it all figured out. Maude is Virgie's and Bessie's half sister. We're her *half* brothers-in-law." Harry frowned from the effort of remembering.

"And we ain't heard from her in years. Read what she says, Hu. That way I can think on it some more."

"That's what I like about you, Harry," Hu said admiringly. "You're a real thinker."

"A what?"

"Thinker, Harry, *thinker!* You're a real thinker." And Hubert smirked while Harry struggled for an answer.

With a rustle of paper Hubert began: "I hope you are both well . . ."

"Skip that part, Hu. Skip where she tells how she moved to Manitoba and how her husband died and all about what she's been doing for 50 years."

Hubert shuffled the pages and began again. "I'm writing, dear Hubert and Harry, to ask a favor. My granddaughter (my son Alexander's girl) needs a place to work. She is a very capable young woman, healthy and strong. Right now things aren't working out well for her here."

"I wonder what that means, Hu."

Hubert shrugged. "Probably an old maid and can't find a husband."

"If she's as pretty as Virgie and Bessie and Maude, that can't be it."

"We'll find out when we see her."

"*If* we see her. We ain't said yes yet."

"Wise up, Harry! We can't get through this winter alone! How high can we let that slop pile get!"

"You're right," Harry acknowledged with a sigh.

"And remember, we prayed the good Lord would send someone."

"You sayin' this what's her name—this Sarah person—is an answer to prayer?"

"Could be, Harry," Hu said stubbornly.

"All right!" Harry capitulated. "So go ahead and write to Maude. Tell her this—Sarah person—can come."

"Me?" The two old men were deep in the throes of the finest wrangle they had engaged in in weeks.

"Hellooo! It's me, uncles!" Carolyn's light voice called, and her slender face peered around the edge of the door.

"Caro! Come on in. You're just the person we want to see." Harry and Hubert exchanged significant glances, rolling their eyes toward the letter, nodding conspiratorially, until Carolyn said, "What are you two up to?"

"Harry and me, we got us a problem," Hubert began, while Carolyn took off her wraps and overshoes.

"Yes," she said, quite aware of their problem.

"Well, our sister-in-law—"

"Our *half* sister-in-law," corrected Harry.

"Virgie's and Bessie's half sister has written us, saying her granddaughter has got herself in some sort of pickle."

"Your grandniece is in trouble?"

"We don't know that, Hu," Harry said testily. "We only know she ain't doin' well where she is. And Maude wants her here."

"What a wonderful idea!"

"Yeah, well, we don't know about that. But we're willin' to give her a chance."

"But we need someone to write the letter for us." Harry and Hubert looked at Carolyn hopefully. She laughed, kissed the weathered cheeks, and rummaged in the desk until she found the necessary materials.

The inane dictation of the brothers swirled over her head as she proceeded to write the distant Maude, telling her of the old men's urgent need of help and their appreciation of having Sarah come and keep house for them. Harry signed it with a flourish, and Carolyn addressed an envelope, sealed it, and promised to see it was taken to the post office.

"She can't possibly get here for a while, maybe weeks," she said musingly. "That gives me enough time . . ." Catching the men's puzzled looks, she flushed and added, "Just thinking, old dears."

Hubert and Harry waited for more.

"I'm going to come more often," Carolyn said firmly, "for a while. You'll need to get this house into shape for a woman to live in it. You'll need to move into one of the bedrooms together (Hubert and Harry looked stricken) and get the other one ready for her. We'll have to get rid of this pile of newspapers, wash the cupboard shelves . . ."

Carolyn took a deep breath, and her eyes glowed. Hubert and Harry blinked, astounded that common housework could be so exhilarating.

"You could've had this pleasure a long time ago," Hu offered helpfully.

Carolyn's laughter was a trill of joy. "Silly uncles!"

Hubert and Harry, for once in their lives, were tongue-tied.

"I'll be back tomorrow," Carolyn said gaily, picking up her coat and clearly forgetting the tasks she had come to do today. "Mum will agree when she hears the reason. She'll agree," she repeated, and muttered as she turned to go. "She just has to."

14

*O*h, Willie, thank you so much!" Abbie took the papers and letter and invited Willie to come in and warm himself.

"No thanks," Willie said, his sweet smile incongruous, as always, in his rough-hewn face. "I have several stops to make. Grandma Dunphy's rheumatism is acting up, and she's been waiting for this delivery of 'Electricating Liniment.' And it looks like Hubert and Harry's long-awaited letter from their grandniece, excuse me—*half* grandniece—has arrived."

Abbie joined Willie's good-humored laugh; everyone in the district knew of the Runyon men's plight and the possible solution to it.

Willie spun away in his light cutter, and Abbie took the mail to the front room, where her mother sewed by the side of the heater and Merry happily cut figures for paper dolls from an outdated catalog.

"It's from Dad," Abbie said, dropping the envelope onto her mother's lap.

Florence laid aside the mending she was doing on the boys' nightshirts and opened the letter. When she had read it, she laid it in her lap. It was obviously the moment they both dreaded.

"Well?" Abbie asked.

"It's time to go home, dear."

"I know," Abbie said stoutly.

"I can't put it off any longer."

"He's been awfully good about it. It's been over six weeks."

Florence's eyes, a little faded in her motherly face, filled with tears. Needed by both her husband and daughter, her place was with her husband.

"Abbie," she said pleadingly, "won't you think over your decision? Come back with me—or follow as soon as you can arrange things here."

"Oh, Mum, don't cry!" Abbie knelt at her mother's side and put her arms around the plump form. Florence was torn emotionally at the thought of leaving her daughter and grandchildren. "I think I'm doing the right thing," Abbie said pleadingly. "And I'm able to do it because you've been here. Don't you see? I was always so afraid of being so far away; now I know you can get here."

"Oh, honey, not really! It's so far—it's such a—a really hard trip. I think if there's any trouble it had better be the other way 'round—you and the children pull up stakes and come to be with your father and me."

"I've got to give it a try, Mum. I think Worth would approve. The children certainly do." Abbie squeezed her mother's hand and rose, to sit opposite her in Worth's curly birch rocker with its comfortable spring-seated, upholstered seat, now an aching reminder of the absent loved one.

"Is your reluctance to leave because Worth is here, dear?" Florence's question was gentle.

"That's part of it," Abbie admitted, thinking of the lonely grave in the Meridian cemetery. "I haven't even had a chance to see the flowers growing on it yet." Abbie's voice was thick with unshed tears. The two women had done their weeping across the weeks they had been together. Now Abbie's tears would be reserved for her private times, making it easier for her mother to leave her.

Florence changed the subject. "You plan to rent the fields?"

"Or have someone work them. That way, we'll be able to keep our home, and it gives us a little money once a year. We don't need much, Mum; we'll raise as much as we can."

"Who will you get to do the work?"

"I talked to Sam. But he has suggested Jamie. I haven't talked to Jamie yet, but I will." Sam had said Jamie was a "born worker" and that he kept busier than ever these days, working from dawn to dark in an effort, Sam supposed, to keep from remembering, or being alone in his empty house.

Florence still looked miserable. "I'll tell you what, Mum," Abbie said. "I'll give it a try until next fall. If things don't work out, we'll come home to Ontario."

Florence sighed. "All right, dear. I'll depend on that." And she went to pack her suitcase.

Winter put on her best display the day Abbie's mother left the bush. As far as the eye could see the world glittered and glistened, sparkled and shimmered. A million and more prisms refracted the sun's beams with scintillating brilliance.

Hoarfrost, like the pelt of a polar bear, thick and white and fluffy, furred every bough. Sound rang on the clear air with the resonance of a struck bell. That gregarious winter bird, the chickadee, puffed its feathery throat with cheerful song: *Chick*adeedeedee . . . *chick*adeedeedee . . .

With winter's grim features momentarily softened, her beauty charmed the weary watchers and waiters, and they remembered that without winter there would be no spring—no return of summer birds, no awakening of the good earth, no sturdy crocus or shy violet—and no hope revived.

Sam and Regina Morris brought the sleigh, and Florence, Abbie, and the children piled in, faces to the wind. Never mind that cheeks would be chapped by nightfall!

From the train, Florence watched the little family bunched on the windswept platform. If there were tears in Abbie's eyes, they were one with the glittering diamonds that flashed a final farewell from the Saskatchewan bush.

*　*　*

When Jamie made his next visit to see how things were going for Abbie and to lend a hand where he could, Abbie called to him, "Jamie, would you mind coming in for a few minutes?"

Jamie unbuckled his overshoes and placed them neatly by the door, hung his cap and coat above them, and relinquished his wet gloves to Abbie to be put in the warming oven to dry as they talked.

Seated in Worth's rocking chair, Jamie recalled the last time he had sat here, when the young widow had so staunchly insisted that she could "manage" by herself. To Jamie's surprise, and his chagrin, she had just about done it. He and Sam had come faithfully, but it was to find wood chopped, the cow milked, the barn mucked out. True, the manure pile at the barn door grew daily, and he wondered grimly what she'd do about that, but he supposed she'd devise a way to get it to the garden spot in the spring. And that was man's work.

The workload, lighter in winter, would increase tremendously with spring—a garden was a necessity, fuel for another winter, baby chicks and other fowl to hatch, perhaps a calf to birth and raise, haying, harvesting.

Jamie's grim expression softened as he watched Abbie settle a small tray on the table and pour tea. There was something about Abbie, he realized, a certain style, that was undeniable. The slim hands were reddened, but graceful. She poured tea with a flair. The angle of her chin, the tilt of her head, the way she moved and wore her clothes all said "class," although Jamie had to grope for the word.

What in the world was she doing, taking on the role of breadwinner? Jamie hoped fervently she was about to tell him she was going to leave the bush; it was the only reasonable solution. But he had heard rumors—

Abbie handed Jamie a fragile cup of fragrant tea and a dainty linen serviette, which he spread over one overalled knee. Cautiously balancing the cup in one big hand, he accepted a generous slice of fruitcake with the other and devoured it in silence.

Abbie seated herself and stirred her tea. "I've decided to stay on," she said.

Jamie's tea threatened to slosh over the edge of the cup.

"You seem surprised," Abbie said, her big amber-colored eyes studying him over the edge of her cup.

"I am—a bit," Jamie confessed, thinking it was the understatement of the year. In truth he was dismayed.

Perhaps his reaction showed. Abbie studied him thoughtfully and said, "You think I shouldn't." It wasn't a question.

"Perhaps." Noting a spark of impatience in Abbie's eyes, Jamie added, "It's your decision, of course. I just feel it's too hard—impossible, really—for a woman alone."

Abbie's eyes glittered dangerously, and Jamie had the idea she was biting her tongue. Fascinated, he watched the struggle; when she spoke, it was to say sweetly, "I'm going to give it a try, Jamie," and Jamie shrugged helplessly.

"Sam hinted at this," he said abruptly, "and hinted you might ask me to take on the farming."

"Are you interested?"

"Yes. And no."

Abbie's eyebrows lifted. "The yes I understand. But the no?"

"I don't fancy working for a woman," Jamie said bluntly. If Abbie wanted to be so independent, she would be treated that way.

Jamie wasn't surprised when anger glowed in Abbie's golden eyes. Until now comparative strangers, they were beginning to get acquainted, and Abbie, Jamie concluded, wasn't liking what she learned any more than he was.

"Well, that's *your* problem," Abbie answered crisply. "This is what I have in mind . . ."

Abbie laid out a businesslike arrangement: Jamie would rent the fields; the responsibility for them would be his, what he planted and when. Payment was due when the crop was harvested—half for her, half for him.

Jamie nodded grimly. Abbie apparently interpreted that as agreement.

"I'll get the team back from Sam," she said.

"Beauty and the Beast."

Abbie looked at Jamie sharply. He kept his face carefully expressionless, and she continued, "That way you won't have to bring your own equipment, or your horses."

"Abbie," he burst out, "if you have the horses here it will mean a lot of work for you!" He wanted badly to add, "Use your head, woman!"

"As expected!" Abbie gritted. "As I said before, Jamie, I'll—"

"Manage!" They spoke the word together, and sat staring at each other defiantly.

Then, "As expected!" Jamie muttered.

Abbie's eyes sparked. Jamie could feel his jaw tightening.

With great politeness, Jamie agreed to the arrangement as outlined and took his departure—but not before he had stiffly accepted a wrapped hunk of fruitcake, stiffly offered by Abbie.

Abbie was both satisfied and exasperated when Jamie had gone. Jamie was exasperated.

15

Willie stepped into the kitchen lean-to, stamped the snow from his big galoshes, spattering snow here and there, and called, "Hey!"

Hubert and Harry craned curious heads from their rocking chairs at the heater's glowing side in the only other downstairs room the log house boasted. "Hey, Willie! Didn't expect you today! C'mon in!"

"Wait a minute 'til I sweep out this mess." Willie's quick swath with the broom swept out not only the snow he had trampled in but also a generous amount of the litter on the Runyon kitchen's faded linoleum. He laid aside his gloves, loosened his collar, and pushed his ear-flapped cap onto the back of his head.

"Take your things off, man, and sit awhile," Harry invited.

"Can't stay. I'm on my way home from town [a figure of speech for the smattering of buildings in the hamlet of Meridian], and I still have some stops to make. But here, I think, is the letter you've been waiting for." With a flourish Willie pulled a battered envelope from an inner pocket.

"Read it, Willie! Sit down and read it!"

"Are you sure?" Willie showed a surprising delicacy.

"We don't have any secrets from you, Willie. Besides, when this Sarah person comes, you'll prob'ly be the one who brings her from the train." Hubert's sly glance checked to see if Willie caught the hint.

It was no surprise to Willie. He opened the envelope, shook out the single sheet, and read: "Dear greatuncles—"

"That's me," Harry couldn't resist singing out. "A great-uncle."

"*Half* great, Harry. And a half-wit to boot!"

Willie continued as though he hadn't been interrupted: "I've agreed to Grandma's plan, with the reservation that I return here next fall if things don't work out."

"Hey! What's this! Don't she want to come?"

"Seems like she'd be dyin' to come look after two old codgers, don't it, Harry?" Hu said scathingly, and Harry subsided.

"After all," Willie read, "you may have a hard time adjusting to a child in the house . . ."

"*What!*" shrilled the brothers.

"She has a child," Willie said calmly. For once in their lives Hubert and Harry were shocked speechless.

"She says," Willie continued, "that she and Simon—"

"Simon."

"I'll be!"

"She and Simon will be here three weeks from today. She supposes you'll have someone at the depot to meet her."

Hubert and Harry raised innocent eyes to Willie, who continued, "She says her grandmother sends her love to you, and she signs it 'Sarah Thrum.'"

"Thrum? Thrum?" Hubert's tone expressed bewilderment. "But that's Maude's name!"

"'Pears there's some kind of problem here, Hu!"

Willie folded the letter thoughtfully and handed it to Harry. "I'll leave you fellas to sort this out," he said soothingly. "If you need help answering it—"

"Yeah, yeah," Hubert mumbled, his mind, obviously, on the "problem."

Harry, more lucid at the moment, said, "Caro's comin' this afternoon."

"Well, she can help you get a letter off. Remember: you don't have to have this—Sarah—come at all if you don't want to."

Willie left, shaking his head with concern for the dismay the two elderly men were feeling and the decision they must make.

The fire popped, and an errant chickadee lit momentarily on the snowy windowsill. But the two old men slouching in their chairs neither heard the cheery sound nor noted the charming guest.

"This Sarah person," Harry said finally, "can't be the answer to our prayer."

"Remember, Harry," Hu said thoughtfully, "remember that we asked for someone *who needs us as much as we need her.*"

Harry groaned.

*   *   *

Hubert and Harry, with a gravity unusual for them, had made their decision by the time a cheery "It's me, uncles!" floated from the kitchen to the fireside where they sat, still wrapped in thought.

"Why so serious, old dears?" Carolyn asked, pressing a cold, rosy cheek to their withered, whiskery faces.

"Caro, this Sarah person is all set to come."

"That's good news, I'd say!"

"You ain't heard it all. There's a—Simon person comin' with her."

Carolyn looked perplexed. "Is that bad news?" she asked.

"This Simon person is a child," Hubert explained glumly.

"But that's wonderful! Tell me, why do you keep saying Sarah person and Simon person?"

"Because their last name is Thrum."

"Well, that is an unusual name, but hardly depressing."

"Oh, it's depressing, all right. Thrum, you see, Caro, is Sarah's grandmother's name—and her father's name. It isn't likely she'd find someone to marry with a name like that too, is it?"

"Oh. Oh!" Carolyn's tone revealed the progression of her thoughts as she assimilated the meaning of this puzzling statement.

"What Hu's gettin' at," Harry said bluntly, "is that the woman is usin' her maiden name."

This time Carolyn said, "Oh, oh," in a small voice and went limp in her chair.

Could Wildrose open its heart to a woman unfortunate enough to be branded with the ultimate disgrace—a child outside wedlock? Although once she would have been swept along with the establishment's opinion of girls who got themselves "in trouble," Carolyn found herself, in her surprising new independence, now saying stoutly, "It won't make any difference to me."

Hubert's next remark laid to rest all doubts concerning the brothers' decision in regard to this unfortunate "Sarah person": "We've been waitin' for you to get here, Caro, to write for us. Tell her—and this Simon child—to come."

With the letter duly written, signed, and tucked into her pocket to be taken eventually to the post office, Carolyn flew about the house, sweeping, washing dishes, straightening papers, polishing the range top, and filling lamps with kerosene.

"I'll be back soon," she promised as she buttoned herself into her coat, "and I'll get to work on your laundry."

"Seems in a turrible hurry today," Hubert remarked when the whirlwind that was Carolyn had swept out the door. "Didn't make no tea—"

"Probably excited because she won't have to make this trip too much longer."

The cutter skidded and jostled down the road, and Carolyn had a little trouble turning the horse to the fainter trail to the lake. Passing earlier, she had glimpsed Micah, just as she had hoped, still cutting ice.

"Turn, you stubborn beast!" she gritted, hauling on the reins until the reluctant mare took the less-traveled track.

Pulling out of the bush, Carolyn stopped the rig at the lakeshore. The red cutter and russet-colored horse made a bright splash against the stark background, and Micah's head turned in Carolyn's direction. Carolyn could see the closed look that came over his face—but not until she had seen the flash of pure joy.

Watching him stride toward her, brow thunderous, Carolyn repressed the laughter that threatened to bubble up. Poor Micah; he couldn't know the forces that were at work. But he would be happy about it yet!

Untutored though she was in the ways of love, Carolyn had instantly recognized the electrifying moment that strikes fire between a man and a woman. Innocent of the practiced ways of the coquette, she knew no better than to respond honestly and forthrightly.

But Micah was harboring some sort of reservation. With the assurance of one who has never been seriously thwarted in life, Carolyn saw it as no problem—a hindrance to be overcome, perhaps, but no lasting problem.

Throwing the lap robe aside, she prepared to step out of the cutter—into Micah's arms. "Don't get out," he said harshly, reaching her side. Carolyn paused.

Standing at the side of the cutter, he looked down at her lifted face, with jaw clenched, eyes stern. It was too much. Her laughter spilled over, and she said gaily, "You don't scare me, Micah Lille. I know you better than you think I do."

Looking sweetly and trustingly up into the handsome, set face, she saw it change; the grim look faded, the harsh expression melted—but only momentarily.

"It's no good, Carolyn."

"It's very good," Carolyn said softly. And if ever lips asked for kissing, hers did.

The black gaze fixed on that vulnerable mouth; Carolyn could almost feel the struggle going on behind the intense eyes. Then they hardened, and the moment was past. "Don't come again, Carolyn."

"But—"

"Don't come again." Micah's lips were tight, but his hands, tucking the robe around her, were unspeakably gentle.

With a quick step he reached the horse and slapped its rump. Startled, the mare leaped forward. Turning the rig, Carolyn headed toward the road, and home.

Passing Micah, she stopped momentarily and said clearly, "I don't understand, Micah. But I will."

The stony-faced man watched her departure with what could only be desperation in his eyes.

16

*J*amie pulled a loaf of bread from the oven and thumped the crust experimentally. Critically judging it satisfactory (but he was so often wrong), he carried it to the table and followed it with three more, thankful they were uniform in size, fragrant to smell, and beautiful to look at. He even managed to get them from the pans without burning himself. And he knew it was important to let them cool before storing them if they were not to turn soggy. Jamie had had enough soggy, fallen, sour bread to last him a lifetime.

That he could manage such jobs at all was due to desperation; there was no one else to do them. And so he doggedly set himself to the tasks necessary for life to go on. But for it to go on pleasantly, even normally, was another thing.

More often than not the household tasks he attempted turned out disastrously. That the bread was a success today was surprising; he didn't understand why it was edible one time and flat and tasteless and gray another time.

Most of his kettles had burned food stuck in the bottom in spite of diligent use of Sapolio Scouring Soap and desperate scrubbings with a scrap of old window screen. The curtain at one window was sagging, and they all needed laundering. To wash them meant to iron them, and Jamie quailed at the thought.

With spring just around the corner, it was obvious he would have to take a morning (a day!) to struggle through the monumental task of washing the rag rugs—rapidly losing their color under layers of dirt—or discard them.

Thinking of washdays, Jamie groaned at the mental picture of the drawerful of blue underwear in his dresser. It was too late now to keep them out of the tub of overalls. Somehow Jamie couldn't bring himself to spread the discolored items over the grass and shrubs as he had seen women do, to let the sun bleach them. As sure as he did, Abbie Rooney would come by (although she had never done so to date) and look superior. Jamie broke into a sticky sweat at the thought.

Cutting a hunk of hot bread and slapping butter on it from a small crock (too salty, he noted grimly) and contemplating these things, Jamie's self-esteem suffered. It hadn't helped any to think of his neighbor, a woman alone, attempting to do a man's job, and doing fairly well at it. But let her face the workload of spring, summer, and fall and see how she'll cope!—no better than he in the kitchen, he imagined, relishing the thought.

The bitter days of winter had slipped away, and now and again there was a hint of chinook weather in the air. Making the trip to the Rooney farm, persistently and stubbornly about twice a week (Sam Morris did the same, on alternate days), it was to find a booted and overalled Abbie hard at work. Aside from a few frozen chickens, all had gone well. When he had rebuilt the ill-fitting henhouse door and sealed up numerous cracks in the chinking, she had thanked him, as she always did at the end of each of his visits, and insisted he take with him a freshly baked dried-apple cake, presenting it to him with as much pride as he had handed over her hammer and saw at the end of his repair job.

The sympathy Jamie had felt for Abbie had changed almost immediately to dismay, and then—having talked with her about her plans—to annoyance. She had given him no reason to better his opinion since.

Why she stayed in Wildrose he couldn't for the life of him understand. He knew she must suffer loneliness; he felt it too. She was unfamiliar with farm life, having been raised in the city. (With chin up, she had silently dared him to laugh at the ribbons on Cinderella's horns, placed there, he supposed, at Merry's request.) Her mother had offered her a home in Ontario, away from the bush she professed to fear. And she feared the bush with just cause, he admitted, for certainly it had been responsible for the death of her husband. Why did she insist on tackling a job she was no more suited to than—than he was to housekeeping!

Jamie balled up the dishtowel and threw it recklessly into a corner of the room, knowing all the while that it would be up to him to rescue it from the dusty spot, fold it, and put it away if it were not to lie there until doomsday.

He was tempted to wrap up a loaf of bread and bear it triumphantly to Abbie, a smug offering prompted by his smarting ego. Instead, he reached for the dishtowel with a sigh, flinching when he caught sight of the greasy butter on it. Now how in the world would he get that out?

* * *

"We almost got 'er made, Harry!" Hubert crowed gleefully. "Spring's as good as here, and we're still percolatin'!"

"You're percolatin' far too happily," Harry growled. "That tonic you've been takin'—"

"'Beef and iron,'" Hu supplied.

"It's far more energizin' than body-buildin', if you ask me!"

"It's the good, hearty beef that's in it, Harry," Hu defended. "It's guaranteed to put color in the cheeks and strength in the muscles, ain't it?"

"You got the color, all right, but the strength all seems to have got lodged in your vocal cords! Go back to Bromo Vichy, Hu. It's a sure cure for 'over brain work,' and yours is showin' signs of stress."

"All I've got is a bilious stomach, and that's because of your cookin'. But soon—," Harry brightened, "we'll have us a real cook! Here comes Caro now, to help us get ship-shape. Things is lookin' up, Hu!"

When Carolyn brought her cleaning materials into the house and outlined the work plan for the day, the brothers agreed to do their share.

Soon the sturdy log house vibrated with activity. Not that Hubert and Harry generated much of it; it was all they could do to navigate. But Carolyn flew around in a flurry of energy, determined to bring order from the chaos of the brothers' careless living and limited abilities. Hubert was to move into Harry's room, and his was prepared for Sarah and Simon.

Hubert, struggling up the stairs with the broom and dustpan, came face-to-face with Harry who, having a good start down with a bundle of laundry, was hard put to halt his head-long flight. Bobbing left and right for a few frustrating moments, they engaged in a brief feinting match; it was the closest they had come in a long time to the scuffling and tussling of past years, as boy and man, and both, obviously, thoroughly enjoyed it. But to admit it was another thing.

"Whoa!" cried Hubert. And legs atremble, they ceased their ineffective efforts to pass on the narrow stairs.

"Whoa yerself, you old billy goat!" retorted Harry with more enjoyment than annoyance. "Can't you see I'm rollin'? Outa my way!" Grateful for a moment to rest, Hubert collapsed against the wall, and his brother made his shaky way to the room below.

"Once up, you gotta come down yerself! If that tonic has kicked in, try the bannisters!" Harry dumped the sour sheets and odorous union suits in a corner, only to pick them up again as Carolyn came in, casting a pained look in his direction. "You'd think the Queen of England was comin'!" he muttered. "I hope her royal highness appreciates all this work!"

"She will," soothed Carolyn, taking the laundry from him. "Why don't you rest a bit, Uncle Harry? You might as well fold these at the same time." She handed him an armload of socks.

Harry sank into his chair and his old fingers fumbled among the woolly assortment until his eyes and his hands coordinated. A thud from overhead drew Carolyn's startled glance upward, and Harry said slyly, "Most likely Hu's collapsed." Carolyn, sure he hadn't but supposing she should make certain, ran for the stairs. As the hem of her skirt twitched out of sight, Harry grinned, put his head back, and closed his eyes.

When Carolyn had picked up the boots Hubert had dropped, she set that gentleman down on the edge of the bed to sort through a drawerful of odds and ends. As he picked up a crochet hook, to cradle it in a hand shaped and misshaped by a lifetime of strenuous work, her eyes misted while his seemed to lose sight of the room's disarray, to fix on a place where she could not follow. With a soft pat to the bent shoulder, Carolyn left the dreamwrapt man, tiptoed past the sleeping Harry, into the kitchen.

Dipping warm water from the range's reservoir, Carolyn made a suds and settled down to scrub the kitchen floor.

*   *   *

Driving over in the buggy (the snow being too scanty for the cutter), Carolyn, heart full of memories, had a clear view of the lake. No manly form strode its edge or bent in labor on its surface. Now ripples were once again riffling the lake edge, and the ice was fast disappearing; bush and tree were free of snow and stretched naked arms toward a sky from which all threat and bluster were gone, and where a sun, long intimidated, was trying tentatively for a comeback.

But Micah Lille was gone.

After he had sent her—with harsh voice and gentle touch—out of his life, she had not seen nor heard from him for weeks. Storms raged as surely in Carolyn's cold heart as through the wintery landscape, and it seemed that this year, more than any other, spring would never come.

But with its first chinook had come the evidence that life still lived, not only in the bush but also in the human heart: Tiger Lille had slipped Carolyn a note at meeting time—"The birches. Three o'clock."

He had been waiting when she arrived, his back pressed gracefully against a tree, one long leg crossed over the other. Straightening, he watched her come, his eyes black as midnight in his expressionless face.

Carolyn stopped only inches from him. With the honesty that had marked all of her contacts with him, she raised her face and looked long into his face. Then, with delightful spontaneity, she laughed, and the sound lifted, happy and free, in the silence of the bush.

"Oh, Micah!" She wrapped both arms around him, and raised her laughing face to his startled face. Laying her cheek on his rough coat, she said softly, "You goose."

Micah drew a deep breath. Then, loosening her arms, he put his own around her, in the first sweet embrace they had known. But he did not kiss her. Holding her gently, and though her willing lips were only inches from his, he did not kiss her.

"Listen to me, Caro," he said, and she listened.

"You're not like other girls I've known," he said. "You're sweet, and you're honest. And you're stubborn. Oh, are you stubborn!"

"I just know what's right for me," she said. "And I know what's right for you," she added, though a mischievous flicker lit her pale eyes.

Micah made a strangled sound that verged on a groan, and his arms tightened.

"I can't be anything but honest with you," he said with quiet determination. "There are things I've got to see about—clear up—"

"You're going back to the reservation." It wasn't a question.

"I have to. And I don't know when I'll be back."

"But you will be back." It wasn't a question.

Another groan. "Oh, Caro! Your strength—do you have enough, I wonder?"

"Mum says I've gotten very headstrong. I call it heart-strong." A smile twinkled in Carolyn's eyes.

"I'm not asking you to wait for me—"

"I'll wait."

Micah's two strong hands gripped Carolyn's upper arms, and he set her aside from him. Black eyes looked deeply, almost desperately, into gray eyes for a long moment.

Micah Lille swung on his heel and strode with purposeful steps through the glistening patches of snow, past the stand of birches, to be enveloped in the bush, and he never looked back.

* * *

When the Runyon brothers' worn linoleum had yielded its sticky patina and some of the original cabbage roses bloomed again, Carolyn dumped the water, took fresh water, and attacked the stove, putting memories aside. Determined to restore the monster range to its former beauty, she polished and cleaned until it gleamed black and silver, and she eyed it with satisfaction, almost convinced it would cook better. At least this "Sarah Person" could approach it now without repugnance.

Refilling the pan, she took fresh towels, soap, and washcloths and carried them upstairs, stopping along the way to wake Harry and urge him to follow.

The brothers, shuddering at the thought of a bath "all over" as much as from the chill of the room, sponged quickly and put on the fresh clean clothes Carolyn had laid out for them.

"Good grief, Harry!" Hubert spluttered, staring at himself in the small mirror over the chiffonier as he combed his hair. "What are you doin' in my lookin' glass?"

"If you'd comb your hair oftener, Hu, you'd reckonize your own self. You're uglier than me."

"But I'm not this old!" objected Hubert.

"You're as forgetful as you are ugly, Hu," said his brother, trying to get a foot high enough to tie his laces, "and you're as ugly as you are old."

"That's your fault! I always did everything you did, Harry, and you, ornery old mule that you are, just kep' on gettin' older and older. Seems I couldn't stop you—and I just tagged along like always."

When his bath was completed, Harry rubbed the brown spots that had appeared as if by magic on the backs of his hands. "I can remember spots like these across the bridge of my nose," he said ruefully.

"Freckles. Virgie had one. Only we called it a beauty spot. Right here on her cheek it was, just by the dimple . . ." The old man's voice trailed off.

But both men brightened when they were seated, clean and warm, by the heater, and Carolyn reported that a chicken was in the oven, potatoes were peeled and ready to boil, and a loaf of fresh bread and some tarts, brought from home, were covered on the sideboard.

"It's worth it already," Harry chortled as he sniffed appreciatively.

Sudden tears in her eyes, Carolyn dropped a quick kiss on the top of each head, scalps ashine through scanty hair, and said good-bye for the last time as keeper of the kitchen. What, she wondered, will I do with my time now? Micah, Micah—hurry back.

Filled with expectation and apprehension, eagerness and reluctance, optimism and misgivings, Hubert and Harry put their heads back.

"Willie'll be bringin' her in an hour or so," Hu said.

"Bringin' *them*, you mean."

*   *   *

With the sun beating ever more warmly on the snow-patched land, men were fixing harness and checking plows, harrows, and seeders; women were bringing up from cellars the last leggy vegetables, grateful to have made it through another winter, and sorting through their supply of garden seeds with another bumper crop in mind.

Abbie, with her skirts hitched up and an old twill jacket over her shoulders, had minced her way around shrinking snowbanks and icy puddles to the patch of ground that, last year, had been tilled by Worth, one of the first tasks he had undertaken upon their arrival in Wildrose. True to its reputation, the soil of the bush was distinguished by its great fertility, high in the essential plant foods and with good moisture-holding qualities. Nevertheless, the undependable growing season could play havoc with garden and crop, shortening the already brief days—perhaps 110 of them—when the area was frost-free. Abbie wanted to get her garden in as soon as possible.

She crouched over the rich black earth among the dead stalks and rotting vegetables lying, stark and ugly, in ragged rows across the plot. The sun was doing its gentle work and coaxing small shoots from the ground, teasing new life from old roots and seeds that had lain dormant all winter.

The lesson was not lost: from last year's abundance, after the worst that winter could do, life's cycle was continuing.

Abbie picked up a handful of the good earth and squeezed it into a damp ball in her hand. She rose to her feet, hearing the awakening world around her, smelling the land, and feeling its life in her two hands.

She filled her lungs with tingling air, dropped the dirt patty, and rubbed her palms on her skirt. "I'll plant the radishes first," she said.

17

*F*or once in his unselfish life Willie had arrived in Meridian without lists from most of the homesteads along the way. That thoughtful gesture was overshadowed by the more pressing consideration for the feelings of the young woman and her child who would arrive weary, perhaps tense, and certainly in no mood to stop at numerous houses on the last leg of their journey, greeting talkative and curious neighbors.

"Picking up the grandniece?" Pete Wiebe asked as he filled Willie's small order and the larger list of the Runyon men, made out by Carolyn Morris in an attempt to replenish their scanty hoard of staples.

Willie nodded, and Pete expected no more. But he watched affectionately as the gaunt man patiently assembled his purchases and took them to his wagon.

"Good man, that Willie Tucker," Pete said to no one in particular. And no one in particular listened.

Willie tied up at the depot, nodded to the station master, and took a seat on an upended barrel, his long legs stretched before him, his boots cumbersome on large feet. He waited patiently.

"Here she comes, right on time," Rudy Bannister, the stationmaster, said as he tucked his watch back into his fob pocket. A distant shriek confirmed his statement, and a cloud of smoke appeared over the top of the bush.

Willie unwound his lanky frame and stood, hands in jacket pockets and an old blue kersey cap set on the back of his black head, as the shining monster burst through the bush and within seconds pulled to a throbbing, steam-punctuated stop.

The conductor swung down, dropped a step, and reached a hand to the woman waiting to descend. She turned to the child who followed at her heels, offering a hand that he ignored in typical boy fashion, jumping to the platform.

This, Willie assumed, was the grandniece and her child, and he found himself somewhat surprised, without knowing why. Perhaps it was that he had been expecting a girl with a babe (the dark insinuations of Hubert and Harry were that Sarah was unmarried). But this was no unformed girl with a shamefaced countenance, carrying an infant. This was a—person—who appeared to be in her early 20s, but with an air of maturity that made her seem older.

This was not the only surprise. In a day when the average female was small, this one was tall and big boned. Here, Willie felt instinctively, there would be no vain pampering of small hands and feet, no dainty posturing, no womanish vapors.

Holding herself erect, almost regally so, the woman's wide, clear gaze swept the platform and fixed on Willie, who had been caught up momentarily in silent curiosity.

"How-de-do, ma'am," he said, stepping forward and removing his cap. "I'm Willie Tucker. I believe your uncles told you I would be meeting your train."

Willie could now see that the eyes were slate gray in color, and very thick-lashed. Her features were strong, the forehead broad, the cheekbones prominent. The nose, though generous, was shapely, and her mouth—wide, full-lipped, richly curved—suited the rest of her face. Willie, never a man given to fanciful thinking and certainly no connoisseur of women, wondered fleetingly what that full mouth would be like when stretched in a smile. He bet himself the teeth would be large, white, and strong. He was not far wrong; he should have added "slightly crooked." But, after her brief smile, her face was composed.

"How do you do, Mr. Tucker," she said in a low voice, and her handshake was firm. "It is good of you to come meet us."

"Not at all," said Willie. "I had to come to town anyway." Another man might have blushed at the remark, but Willie was his honest, unpretentious self.

If the woman was a moment too long in answering, Willie didn't notice, but her gaze was serious, her look intent. Then, "This is my son, Simon," she said quietly, placing her hand on the child's head. Her hand, like the rest of her, though large, was beautifully boned and shapely, giving the appearance of great capability. Willie's fears concerning her ability to cope with the situation at the Runyon household suddenly shrank to manageable size.

The boy's eyes lifted to Willie's face and, like his mother's, were large, gray, and thickly lashed. But where hers were cool and distant, his were soft and sensitive. And his face, rather than strong and composed, was slender—like the mysterious man who fathered him, Willie supposed fleetingly. The boy's hair, under the edge of his cap, was thick and fair where his mother's, caught in a loose knot at the back of her head, was a deep honey color.

"Hello, son," Willie said, and the boy's eyes flickered as he stared up at the towering figure. Willie's mirror told him of his craggy features, deep-set eyes, and mournful expression, and he well knew his face settled automatically

into lugubrious lines and that only his occasional smile relieved what he had been laughingly told was a dour appearance. Now he smiled.

"You look like—," the boy said impulsively.

"Abraham Lincoln."

The boy's eyes widened.

"Simon," the mother said gently.

"It's all right, ma'am," Willie said, and smiled again.
"I've been told it often enough." No one, it seems, had ever
bothered to tell him that he was also singularly like that
historic figure in quality as well as in looks.

With Rudy's help, Willie loaded the baggage that had
been set beside the woman's feet and, at his invitation,
Sarah stepped lightly to the wheel hub and up into the
wagon; Simon clambered aboard by himself.

Seated between the two adults on the high spring seat,
the small child was quiet—perhaps shy, perhaps tired—
and the woman almost equally so. There was no nervous
chatter, no trivial conversation, and no questions as they
made their way out of Meridian and toward Wildrose. This
suited Willie perfectly. Willie found conversation—particularly light, meaningless chitchat—difficult at all times, and
especially so where a stranger was concerned, and a
woman at that.

Willie put his big paw into his jacket pocket, winked
down at the child, and dropped a paper sack into the small
hand that reached spontaneously for it. The sensitive gray
eyes warmed as they looked up at the big man.

The horses plodded on, the wagon creaked and
bounced, and the gaze of the boy held the gaze of the man
as only a child's can—steady, serious, unselfconscious—
until Willie, strangely moved and not knowing why,
tugged the reins, spoke urgently to the team, and they
broke into a trot.

144 • *Ruth Glover* •

How was a childless bachelor to know there was something more than mere lemon flavoring and sugar in the golden globe the boy transferred to his mouth? How could an empty-hearted and overlooked man know that embodied in a small gift was an ingredient that, given time and opportunity, would sweeten three lives?

"Giddap!" said the man gruffly.

"Giddap!" echoed the small voice in a burst of joy.

18

*H*ubert and Harry had worked themselves into a fever of curiosity, anxiety, and impatience before Willie delivered Sarah and Simon, deposited their belongings inside the door, and drove away, leaving them to handle what they anticipated would be a tense situation.

Sarah greeted her granduncles with a natural simplicity, hung her wraps and the child's behind the kitchen door as though she had done it all her life, turned to the two hovering men—usually so loquacious and now so tongue-tied—and said, matter-of-factly, "I'll just take our things to our room."

"Upstairs . . . ," Harry managed, and made a convulsive move in the direction of the stairs.

"I'll find it."

The child followed her, glancing shyly at the two elderly men from lowered lids. Hubert and Harry, as in all times of stress, collapsed into their ancient rocking chairs.

"Uh, so far, so good, I guess you could say," Hu offered in a low voice.

Harry swallowed, and whispered, "Sort of—buxom, wouldn't you say?"

"Well, she ain't no sparrow, Harry. But she ain't no pouter pigeon, neither."

Silence reigned until Sarah came back down the stairs, the child in tow. Pausing at her uncles' chairs, she said,

"Smells like dinner is in the oven. I'll see to it." And she made her way to the kitchen, Simon hugging her heels.

Alert to the sounds and smells emanating from the kitchen, Hubert and Harry, by turn, rolled expressive eyes at each other when the oven door opened, picked up their ears when bread was sliced, nodded knowingly when boiling water was poured into the teapot. And when Simon appeared in the doorway and announced that supper was ready, they made their self-conscious ways into their own kitchen and took their places, feeling strange, at their own table.

Clearly this Sarah wasn't a talker. Neither, at least tonight, was the boy. Simon's cheeks turned rosy over his plate, and his eyelids dropped from weariness. Finally Sarah excused herself and took the child off to bed.

Before she returned to the cleanup tasks, Hubert and Harry, belts tight after the best meal they had eaten in a long time, escaped once again to their fireside retreat, to the sounds of a woman—once again—doing the homey things a woman does so well and which they had missed so much.

With her apron removed, running her hand through her abundant hair and tucking back a stray lock or two, Sarah stepped into the room where four anxious eyes were lifted to her; a small smile touched her lips and her eyes softened.

"I won't stay down with you tonight, if you'll excuse me. It's been a long day."

About to leave, she turned, and the gray eyes were shadowed. "I want to say, though," she said softly, "that Simon and I thank you for taking us in."

With that she mounted the stairs. Behind her she left, staring after her, four blank eyes and two faces with dazed expressions.

"Did you hear that, Harry?" Hu's whisper broke the silence. "*She* thanks *us!*"

"I'll be!" Harry's dropped jaw confirmed his amazement. "Fancy that, Hu. *Her*—thankin' *us!*"

"Looks suspiciously like God workin' in mysterious ways His wonders to perform!"

It was enough to set the two brothers to much whispered speculation, until the fire burned low and the room chilled, and they realized they had gone past their bedtime. After banking the fire, they took a lamp and crept up to the room they were to share.

Although they tugged at the covers and muttered dire threats to each other concerning staying on the proper side of the bed, even this aggravation faded before the comfort of knowing someone else was in the house and that there would be a warm breakfast in the morning with a couple of bright faces at the table.

To think of it! Sarah needed them as much as they needed her.

"This praying business, Harry," Hubert said sleepily, "sure pays off!"

"Could get to be a habit," his brother allowed.

*   *   *

Following the anticipated breakfast of hot oatmeal (Sarah had left it soaking in a pot on the range all night), great drafts of yellow cream mixed with brown sugar, toast (not burned!), and coffee—good coffee—Hubert and Harry shoved back from the table, shuffled to the hooks behind the door, and shrugged themselves painfully into their coats.

Hubert picked up the water pail, dumped the remaining contents into the reservoir, and turned his steps toward the well, and Harry tottered to the woodpile and began strenuous efforts at chopping wood.

Sarah was waiting on the porch to take the pail of water and to help with the armload of wood that teetered in Harry's stringy arms, her mouth set in a firm line.

After brushing the sawdust from Harry's coat and hanging up their wraps, she led the men, atremble from the exertion, back to the sanctuary of their chairs and the cushions permanently shaped to fit their individual proportions.

Now, dandled comfortingly in the embrace of their rocking chairs and the cushions made by Bessie and Virgie years ago and indented to fit, Hubert's and Harry's squalling was hushed by the final cups of coffee Sarah brought to them.

"Uncles," she said, and they raised rheumy eyes to her face, "I'll get the wood and water from now on." And being in no position to back good intentions with good performances, Hubert and Harry could only bluster.

"We ain't used to a woman waitin' on us hand and foot!"

"We're perfectly able to—" Harry's voice trailed off, knowing they were not able at all.

If a smile twitched at the corners of the woman's generous mouth, who could say on such short acquaintance? "It's what I'm here for," she said briefly, and that settled that.

But when she returned to the kitchen, Harry turned to his brother and hissed, "It don't seem right!"

"Cookin's one thing—choppin' wood's another, while we sit here like bumps on a log!"

But the logs were comfortable, and the "bumps" knew their own helplessness and pondered on it, dismayed and delighted at the same time.

"I've got it!" Hubert yelped suddenly, and Harry's coffee sloshed.

"We'll see if Willie'll help!"

"Yeah—he owes us a favor!" Harry's response was sarcastic.

"Well no, but he's a good Christian and all. Don't the Good Book say if thy neighbor's water pail is empty, fill it? And blessed is he that choppeth his neighbor's wood?"

"Something like that," Harry admitted.

"Aw, Willie'll do it. You know if we ask Willie for his coat, he'd give us his cloak also."

And Harry knew he would.

When Willie made his next trip with their fresh supply of milk and eggs, Hubert and Harry asked him to come in and "sit a spell." Aware of urgency in their tones, Willie laid aside his coat, sat down by the fire, and looked at the old eyes fixed cunningly on him.

"You're a good man, Willie."

Willie's expression turned cautious.

"We was just thinkin', Harry and me, about how many stars you're bound to have in your crown—"

"Something I can do for you, fellas?"

"Here's a man, Harry, that truly loves his neighbor as hisself!"

Willie, a patient man, recognized the guile of these old men, no longer able to live by their own sweat and muscle, and he appreciated the wit that never forsook them. So he waited for the little drama to come to its conclusion. Sarah, standing at a small table pouring tea for her uncles and their guest, seemed to repress a smile.

It would be a small effort on Willie's part, Hubert explained, and it would be a big favor to them and their little grandniece (Sarah's head lifted) if he would take a moment—well, several moments—when he was here anyway, to lug in extra wood and water.

Sarah set the teapot down abruptly.

Persuasion was not necessary; Willie was agreeable. "Be glad to help," he said, and the brothers shot triumphant glances at each other. Sarah poured and served the tea thoughtfully.

The truth was that Willie was experiencing a sense of relief where the Runyon men were concerned. Although the preacher called on them and Carolyn helped with the housework, he, Willie, was the only one who had regular contact with the elderly men, and concern over their frailty was ever with him. Already some of the burden was lifted in the arrival of their grandniece. He would gladly assist.

At the door, ready to leave, Sarah held out the empty, clean milk can and she said firmly, "There's no need for you to take on more responsibility for my uncles, Mr. Tucker. I am prepared to take over the tasks they just asked you to do."

Once again Willie said the ungallant, but honest, thing. "I'll be over here anyway, bringing the milk."

From his towering height he looked down on the woman—girl, he supposed—revising his first opinion. So quiet, so self-contained, she seemed older than she was. Whatever her age, she was a woman, and no girl.

Sarah's eyes, cool in their bed of lashes, studied Willie's face, a face Willie well knew for its gaunt cheeks, large nose, broad forehead. "Abraham Lincoln," the boy had said, and Willie didn't think it flattered Mr. Lincoln. How could he know that his eyes were gentle, and his lips, over very white teeth, were unusually sweet for a man? No one, no one at all, had ever told him so.

Sarah didn't pursue the matter of the chores, but Willie had an idea she would quietly and efficiently do them herself. She thanked Willie and stepped back, her forearms gleaming below rolled-up sleeves, shapely hands planted easily on generous hips. Even Willie's unpracticed eye noted that above them the apron was knotted around a very trim waist. He looked hastily away and very nearly blushed. Fumbling with the milk can, he murmured his good-byes.

*   *   *

With a reluctant Simon by the hand, Sarah trudged under a chilly spring sky to the Wildrose school, pleased to have found it was just over the brow of the hill and across the road. With only a few weeks of school remaining in the year, she felt it was best to enroll Simon, to acquaint him with the teacher, and help him begin to feel at home, perhaps make a few friends. Certainly it would make it easier in the fall.

A tall and fresh-faced youth greeted her and introduced himself. "Good morning! I'm Ben Fairchild, the teacher—at least for a while." He smiled warmly, and it was impossible not to smile back.

"I'm Sarah Thrum," Sarah said, "and this is Simon." She drew the fair-haired, slender-faced child forward. Twenty pairs of eyes were raised from as many desks as Wildrose children studied the new pupil.

"Come up to my desk, Mrs. Thrum, and we'll get a little information from you and find a desk for Simon."

"It's Miss Thrum." The woman's eyes were fixed steadily on the teacher's.

"The young man stammered, "You are Simon's—"

"Mother."

Ben Fairchild's ruddy face flushed ruddier still. To recover his poise he busied himself with paper and pencil. Age? Seven. Grade? Two.

When Sarah left, Ben was putting Simon's material in one of the small front desks, and Simon, more pale than usual, was standing tensely at his side, eyes on the floor.

With a sigh, Sarah closed the door and strode across the road, through the fence and down the hill, toward a house that she could not call home, housing two men—

neither of them husband to her or father to the child she left behind in the quiet room.

The overcast sky was no grayer and scarcely more bleak than the eyes fighting for their usual cool, self-controlled look.

19

rue to the deal he had made, Jamie plowed the Rooney garden. Abbie hovered at the edge of the patch, obviously eager to get it planted.

Pulling the team to a halt at her side when he was through, he said, "I'll be over in the morning to help with the planting."

"Thank you, Jamie," she said, coolly, sweetly, "but I'll manage."

A dull red crept up from Jamie's open shirt collar to stain his face, winter-white behind its shaggy black mustache and beneath an equally shaggy black head of hair, and he growled, "I'll be here in the morning!"

And he was, to find Abbie's slim form bent over a hoe raking, clearing, and leveling and the children cheerfully helping.

Taking a hoe, Jamie wordlessly scooped his way, hole by hole, across one end of the patch. If Abbie had a different area in mind for the potatoes, she kept it to herself and followed meekly enough, dropping chunks of potato into each hole, while the boys covered the hills.

Without stopping, Jamie put up stakes and string and marked out straight rows for beans, peas, turnips, lettuce, and radishes. If he noticed Abbie's regressively tightening lips, he kept it to himself.

Finally, swinging the hoe unnecessarily viciously, he chopped a few weeds here and there and tramped off toward the team and the fields. Abbie's eyes, he felt certain, were on his back and probably filled with something of the fury he felt.

He was mollified to some degree, however, when she called after him, "Thank you, Jamie," only to be infuriated anew when she added, "Let me know when you're doing your garden, and the children and I will come and help."

With what he thought was a master stroke, he flung over his shoulder, "I'll manage!" But a flush of shame replaced the flush of anger when he saw Corcoran and Cameron, with puzzled faces, look from their mother to him, and back again.

* * *

With a few weeks of backbreaking, sunburning, hand-callousing work behind them, Wildrose was ready for a break. Hearts lifted when Brother Victor announced the yearly Sunday School picnic. Committees were appointed, menus were planned, and schedules were arranged and re-arranged for this, the official opening of summer.

To Jamie's knowledge, Abbie had not attempted to harness and hitch the team to the wagon. For the trip to church she and the children walked to the Morris farm and rode with them.

If truth were told, Jamie's kind heart struggled with his impatience with Abbie, and he felt he should offer to take her and the children to the picnic; after all, he would go right by their place. But feeling uncomfortably sure he would be rejected out of hand, he couldn't bring himself to mention it.

One afternoon, unhitching the horses in her barnyard, he was surprised to hear Abbie's voice at his shoulder. "Jamie, I've been thinking about the picnic. You'll be going, won't you?"

"Why, sure," he said, prepared to respond magnanimously to her need for transportation.

"Well," she said sweetly, "I'll be happy to take food enough for you, so you won't have to try to make anything—like bread."

How did she know about his bread-baking efforts! Although his neck burned, Jamie managed a strangled, "I'm perfectly able to prepare something. Thank you, anyway."

"But I can just as well fix a little extra," she pursued.

If he hadn't looked at her he might have come off better. But noting a decided quiver to her lips, he burst forth with a second, "I said I'll—"

"Manage!" She beat him to it, laughter definitely spilling from the depths of her amber eyes.

Jamie yanked at the traces, hastily making his escape, wishing with all his heart he had come up with something original.

Subsequently, he had struggled through one fallen cake, a burned pie, and tough fried chicken. With near desperation he thought of deviled eggs, and with grim satisfaction turned out an acceptable platter full, loaded his box—eggs, one plate, one cup, one set of silverware, one denim-stained serviette—and left for the picnic.

Passing Abbie's gate, he saw her—straight and slim, cool and radiant, in a white dress, the first he had seen her wear (aside from Sunday mornings) in a long time—putting her things in the Morris wagon.

Seeing her garbed as she was in Worth's trousers so often, Jamie had forgotten how womanly Abbie was; the reminder served to bring him to a boil again as he fumed at her ridiculous (he thought) stab at independence. He, of all people, should know the foolishness of her undertaking. He, more than any other, suffered pangs of remorse over another such arrangement.

Refusing to think that Dora might, after all, have borne up under their emergency, Jamie had taken on himself a heavy burden of guilt. But Abbie's tenacity and courage threatened his viewpoint, and he resisted the possibility of shifting blame that, he stubbornly insisted, was his.

"Impossible woman!" he muttered as he passed. "Can't she see the job's too big for a woman?"

Abbie watched Jamie drive past and waved airily, gnashing her teeth at the same time. Although sympathetic with his grief (who understood it better than she?), Abbie had little or no patience with Jamie's relentless self-castigation.

"Impossible man!" she gritted. "Can't he see the uselessness of it?"

*   *   *

An unenthusiastic Carolyn climbed down from the wagon and helped carry the food boxes to the tables that were already groaning under Wildrose kitchens' best efforts: Grandma Dunphy's saskatoon pie, Regina Morris's raisin tea cakes, Mary VanVleeks' oliebollen. Each cook had her specialty, always expected and always forthcoming.

And perhaps most yearned for of all—bowls of crisp lettuce, a delicacy almost forgotten during the long winter months of canned vegetables and withered potatoes and turnips.

But food held no interest for Carolyn, whose pale face was more wan than usual after a housebound winter. And she looked without relish toward the group of chattering girls gathering near a group of young men. Soon, she knew, the two groups would meld into one, and then break up into couples who would gaze soulfully into each other's eyes, say provocative things, and, if bold enough, hold hands.

Contemplating the day with apathy, Carolyn's sighs were silenced when the Lille wagon rolled into the meadow, Joe holding the reins, and beside him on the spring seat, Ruby and Tiger. And on Ruby's comfortable lap was a small girl, black head shining in the sun, skin dusky, eyes shy, a finger in her rosy mouth.

Startled, Carolyn watched as Tiger leaped with her usual grace to the ground and reached slender arms for the child. Obviously proud of the little one, Tiger took a dimpled hand in hers and moved toward the table area and the women working there or seated nearby. As one person, the women of Wildrose, to whom any newcomer was an immediate object of interest, silenced their chatter and watched.

"Who have you got there, Tiger?" boomed Grandma Dunphy, holding her trumpet to her ear.

Tiger's reply was lost to Carolyn and apparently to Grandma Dunphy also. "Speak up, girl!" she shouted, certain everyone was as hard of hearing as she was.

As Tiger leaned toward the trumpet, Gabe Durham stopped strumming his mandolin, and Tiger's words carried clearly to Carolyn: "This is Cheri."

"So," bellowed Grandma Dunphy curiously, "who does this Cherry belong to, eh?"

"Micah," Tiger said, the sound echoing in the well of silence. "Cheri is Micah's daughter."

The words reached Carolyn with the force of a thunderbolt.

* * *

The church ladies, at the rear of the tables, doled out mouthwatering portions to any plate held in their direction. In line, Jamie eyed food such as he had almost thought never to taste again. His eggs, he noted with satisfaction like any cook, were disappearing as quickly as the others.

Giving his best pair of pants a hitch ("We guarantee that if a pair rips or a button comes off, or when the garment is found defective, we will replace it free of charge") around his middle, Jamie noted they were looser than before and that his lean frame was definitely leaner than ever. Why he didn't spend more time and effort on his meals he didn't know; it was boiled potatoes or boiled beans all the time. Now he skirted both, moving on to more tempting dishes.

Catching sight of Abbie Rooney behind the next table, Jamie fingered a small tear in his blue chambray "never-rip" shirt and wished fervently he had taken time to mend it. The "good, solid-woven fabric known the world over for its excellent wearing qualities" had succumbed readily to a tangle with a barbed wire fence.

Sure enough, Abbie's eyes were fixed on the rip. Watching her with defensive eyes, Jamie saw Abbie's gaze move from the rip to his face, and the golden glance—usually as full of sparks as a bonfire—softened.

"When you've got what you want, Jamie," she said, her tone surprisingly gentle, "go and sit down and eat. I'll bring dessert when you're ready for it."

"You mean," Jamie said warily, "you'll give me my just desserts?"

Abbie's laugh was spontaneous, and she answered, as the impatient line of people pushed him on, "No, Jamie. But your plate is full. I'll bring another one, with your dessert. What do you like? Pie, cake, tarts—"

"All that," he called back. "Anything but taters and beans!"

When the sun began its slide toward the west, every man, with one mind, turned his thoughts toward the evening chores and his feet toward the line of wagons.

Every woman called her children, collected her things, followed her man to their rig, and bade her friends a reluctant good-bye.

Soon only a few young people were left at the lakeside, wandering hand in hand through the lengthening shadows, tossing pebbles into the water, watching for the moon to come up, and dreaming dreams only the young and innocent can dream.

Jouncing miserably on the spring seat as the wagon made its uneven way across the meadow, Carolyn cast a final glance at the Lille group and the tired child—dark head dropping, dark eyes closing—in Tiger's arms. Holding blindly to the thought that had sustained her thus far, she thought fiercely, "He said he'd be back, and he is. I said I'd wait, and I will! But oh, Micah—Micah—"

* * *

Abbie was in a quandary. She had come with the Morrises, but when they were ready to leave, Corky and Cammie were nowhere to be found. "Go ahead," Abbie told Regina. "I'll catch a ride with someone."

The children eventually made their appearance. Studying the remaining group for a possible ride, Abbie's eyes met Jamie's.

"I'd offer to help," he said cautiously, "but I feel quite sure you're going to manage somehow. Do you mind if I watch?"

Abbie flushed, but—finally—she threw up her hands in mock resignation, and said, "I admit it. I need help." Her audible aside, "this time," was overheard by an incredulous Jamie, who shook his head and received a half-defiant look in return.

But it seemed good to her to have a man's strong arms lift the box she struggled with, as though it contained chicken feathers; it seemed natural to have long male legs stride beside her, two steps to her one. Abbie admitted (to herself, and only briefly) that it was a grim battle to cope alone.

With the weary children settled sleepily in the back of the wagon, Abbie and Jamie rode home through the late afternoon, in companionable conversation, a truce struck, temporarily at least.

20

Summer—with its heat, its flies, its mountain of work—was in full swing. Joyously abandoning long-handled winter underwear, symbol of the northlands, children felt liberated from the stricture of school, house, weather, and wraps and roamed the woodlands and meadows, climbed trees to destroy crows' nests, poured slough water down gopher holes, and picked and ate wild strawberries until their rosy mouths stained redder still.

Even for them some work was inevitable. But can berry-picking be work when the sun is warm on bare arms, bees hum at one's elbow, chipmunks scurry overhead, and there is a promise of gooseberry fool or pin cherry sauce or saskatoon pie for supper? The misery of weeding the garden was eased by the sure realization that meals of creamed new potatoes and peas were forthcoming. Chicken feeding was a pleasure when golden balls of fluff followed at the heels ("Ma, do chickens have heels?") of the hens, to pick at small, bare toes and hop on sunburnt insteps. Driving cows to pasture was pure fun when small calves gamboled alongside and the cowbell sang a tinny tune into the glorious morning air. Wildrose children reveled in summer.

As for their mothers, they worked from sunup to sundown, and then some. Nothing must go to waste from the garden; though it meant long, hot hours of canning, it was insurance against a winter of skimpy meals. Heavy quilts, saturated with months of human contact, were clumsily laundered while the sun blazed strongly enough to dry them, and winter's grim chill was checked. New bed sheets, made from unbleached muslin, were laid for days on the grass and over the bushes to bleach and soften, and the best portions of worn linens were cut into tea towels, dishrags, and dustcloths; nothing was discarded in the bush until the last scrap of use had been wrung from it.

Little lean-to kitchens palpitated with heat. Scarcely a meal was eaten without a roaring fire in the range; not a dish could be washed, not a bath taken, not a cup of tea steeped without it. The family wash required a boiler of steaming water; bread had to be baked once, even twice, a week. In summer, aprons were used as often to swipe sweaty brows as to protect gingham house dresses. But slowly, and satisfyingly, homes regained a sweet, fresh smell, rooms brightened with a snowy coat of whitewash, windows sparkled once again, and cellars filled with a supply of food.

Taking a breather from the hot kitchen and the rows of canned beans cooling on the table, Carolyn stepped outside, around the corner of the house, and into the shade of a stand of poplars. Leaning against a tree, thinking (as usual) about Micah and the child Cheri, and desperately searching for answers, a prayer at long last lifted from her heart.

Heavenly Father, this feeling I have for Micah Lille—I'm not strong enough or wise enough to handle it. I turn it over to You . . .

As she released tears that needed to flow, peace flooded the heart that had been so despairing and quieted the mind that had been so awhirl.

Why didn't I do this long ago? she wondered and knew the answer. Glorying in an awareness of inner strength (though her body was frail), she had overlooked "from whence cometh" that strength. Now, acknowledging its source as "the Lord, which made heaven and earth," her tipping world righted. "Thy word have I hid in mine heart," Wildrose Sunday School children recited and, year after year, 52 scripture verses were hidden in small hearts. Now one had been there when needed.

Picking up the corner of her spattered pinafore, Carolyn wiped her eyes, breathed shakily, and turned toward the house with lighter feet than had carried her to the place of prayer.

*   *   *

There was no way around it; Hubert's and Harry's odorous bedding had to be washed.

Hard work was no stranger to Sarah. But quilt washing made even her strong spirit quail. First there was the monumental task of carting numerous pails of water from the well to the house, to be lifted to the copper boiler on the range. When that was hot it had to be lugged, pail by steaming pail, to the galvanized tub she set up in the yard. One by one the wool-pieced, wool-stuffed quilts were crammed into the tub and soap shavings added, followed by a mighty stomping with the metal funnel fixed to a broom handle.

But all this was nothing compared to the almost impossible task of wringing the mountainous bulk free of water and soap, with the whole thing to be done over in rinse water. It was arm-aching, backbreaking, breathtaking work.

Halfway through and already worn to a frazzle, Sarah paused and leaned wearily on the stomper over the final rinse to feel a hand on her shoulder and a compassionate voice say, "Here—I'll take a turn."

It was Willie, of course.

Numbly turning over the stomper, Sarah sat down on an upended laundry basket, more grateful than she had words to express. But already she knew they weren't expected; Willie was Willie.

Nevertheless, she had to try. When the last water-logged item had been squeezed and wrung until it was manageable, heaved onto Willie's shoulder, and trundled to a springy patch of goose grass and spread to dry, Sarah said a warm, "Thank you, Willie. Thank you so much!" and it seemed to be enough.

"*Willie!*"

Simon and his pup, Scratch, a recent gift from Willie, burst from the shadows of the empty barn. Simon had been climbing the stalls, clambering in the mangers, swinging from the frayed rope, and all with the cavorting, yapping, flop-eared dog at his heels. Skidding to a halt inches from the big man, he asked breathlessly, "Me and Scratch—can we go with you today?"

"Simon—," Sarah murmured.

"Let him come, Sarah," Willie said gently, and she did.

Hand in hand, the man and the boy walked to the wagon, heaved in the dog, climbed in, and rattled out of the yard. "Me and Willie are takin' cream to town," Simon shouted. "Then we're gonna deliver mail to ever'body all the way home."

"Talking more and more like the uncles," Sarah thought, "and acting more and more like Willie." And in neither instance did she feel like interfering.

* * *

Abbie was hauling up a pail of water when she heard a thud, and she looked around to see Cinderella stepping over a just-flattened fence post.

"Corky! Cammie! Get that cow out of the garden!"

When there was no response, Abbie remembered that the boys had gone gopher hunting, followed by their dog and their sister, in that order.

With her eyes and thoughts on the cow now munching her way toward the tender lettuce, Abbie set the pail down hastily; too late she saw it tip from the lip of the well and fall back into its dark depths. Already turning to spring toward the garden, she groaned, "Oh, no!" The end of the rope was unfastened; she saw it follow the pail out of sight. It didn't help her vexation.

Snatching up a handful of clods, Abbie pelted the pesky cow, now watching her with liquid eyes while lettuce disappeared into her working jaws.

"Git! Git—you *creature* you!" Maddened by its very docility, she yelled at the beast, and it began a slow amble toward the barnyard.

Not satisfied, Abbie followed, dancing in rage, shooing and calling names and wishing she could deliver a swift kick to the plump rump under which the heavy udder tossed ridiculously as the animal finally broke into a shambling trot.

Wearily she turned to survey the damage: a fence post down and the barbed wire with it—as if she didn't have enough to do!

There were times when Abbie wished with all her heart she was sitting in her living room in Ontario—carefree and tranquil, far removed from the bush—with her well-coifed head filled with nothing more serious than which dainty sandwich to choose, and with a cup of fragrant tea in a hand on which the fingernails were freshly buffed, exchanging pretty comments with an afternoon visitor. But that seemed a lifetime away as she stood— booted feet apart in goose grass, calloused palms planted on overalled hips, perspiration trickling in rivulets over her dusty forehead from beneath the edge of Worth's old felt hat, with gentle conversation forgotten for the tongue-lashing of a dull bovine.

Shutting her eyes, she prayed fervently, *"Give me strength!"*

"Ye ask, and receive not, because ye ask amiss," quoted a male voice behind her.

Abbie whirled to see Jamie, also surveying the broken fence and the trampled garden. "You should have a pulpit, Jamie! I didn't know you had a license to preach!" she said scorchingly.

"There are lots of things about me you don't know." And although he didn't add "Miss Smarty Britches," his tone implied it.

With Abbie almost visibly palpitating with hostility and exasperation, Jamie went to the fence and raised the fallen post only to have it fall again the moment he let go of it.

Caught in a defenseless moment and smarting because of it, Abbie looked at the ruin the cow had wrought and at the strong male creature who had caught her in a lapse into weakness, and in spite of herself a huge tear welled up in her eyes, trembled behind hastily lowered lashes and, at last, betrayed her by slipping slowly down her cheek. Turning her head she swiped furtively at her face, bent and fumbled with her shoelaces, dusted her trousers, and, finally, settled her emotions enough to face Jamie and say, brightly, "So! Another challenge!"

Crouched on his heels beside the fallen post, Jamie looked up from his inspection of the rotted base and studied the disheveled young woman. Since their ride home together from the picnic, an armistice of sorts had existed between them, and because of it and the clear-eyed look Jamie was giving her now, Abbie's defenses, already weakened, slipped still further.

To her horror—in front of Jamie's watching eyes—a second tear welled. The miserable drop swelled until, fat and translucent, it spilled over.

The end of the little drama might have been totally different if Jamie had had the wit to take her in his arms. Instead, he got to his feet, and black anger darkened his eyes. "You had absolutely no business taking on a job of this size! I told you that in the first place! But would you listen? No, you knew best!" Jamie's frustration also found an outlet and boiled to the surface.

Abbie blinked, and Jamie continued furiously, "Look at you!" And his eyes raked her from dusty hat to dusty boots.

Abbie's eyes wavered and fell to her hands; she turned them over and studied them. Jamie stepped swiftly to her and grasped her small hands in his big ones, holding them up for the inspection of both of them. "What are you trying to do to yourself?" His voice was rough.

Abbie pulled her hands free and stuffed them in her pockets. But Jamie wasn't finished; he snatched the old hat from her head and ran a contemptuous hand through her hair. It tumbled down around her face, stray tendrils clinging to the cheeks dampened by sweat and tears.

"Half man, half woman!" he muttered. "It's not natural!"

Abbie swallowed and backed off. Jamie followed. Wiping a finger across her cheek, he looked at the combination of tears and dust that muddied it and grunted, "Some face powder!" His foot nudged the boot on her slender foot, caked with the muck of the barn. "*Eau de Manure!* toilet water! Real toilet water, Abbie!"

Wide-eyed but speechless before this tirade, Abbie finally rallied. "You—you *man*, you!" she cried, in much the same tone she had used earlier when she had castigated the cow.

"Yes! That's right!" Jamie said emphatically. "A man! And just what you aren't, nor ever will be! And just what is needed around here! That's what you should be praying for—a man, and a man's strong right arm!"

Abbie's mouth flew open, but he continued, "Dress like a man if you will! Smell like one if you must! But for Pete's sake, quit trying to act like one!"

Step by step, Abbie had retreated before Jamie's hot eyes and prodding finger, and all remembrance of his kindness since Worth's death fled from her thoughts. Forgotten was his gentleness with Merry, who ran to have him lift her onto the broad backs of Beauty and the Beast, sliding off into his arms, clinging around his neck until he tickled her loose. Forgotten were his rough-and-tumble play with the boys, the times he took them for rifle practice, and the coppers he doled out when he took them with him to the store.

Finished backing up, Abbie dug in her heels. Still advancing, Jamie shouted, almost in her ear. "A woman— alone! You can't keep this up!"

Jamie almost bumped into Abbie and, looking flustered, stopped with his chest inches from her stubborn dusty nose. The sight of a few freckles, never seen before this summer's work, obviously did nothing to cool his passion.

Somewhat disadvantaged by her position but refusing to budge further, Abbie stood her ground, and Jamie, by now a bit abashed, fell back, muttering darkly.

"And so," Abbie said in an ominous voice, "you would have me pray for a man."

"Abbie—" Jamie suddenly seemed inspired to offer an answer to a prayer that hadn't been uttered, "I volunteer!"

Confronted by her dumbfounded expression, Jamie calmed himself, took Abbie's unresisting hand and led her to the well, seating himself on the raised wooden frame and drawing her down beside him. Abbie had a momentary uneasy thought for the missing pail and rope, hoping Jamie wouldn't notice their absence.

Wiping a beading of perspiration from his brow, Jamie said, as sensibly as though he were discussing the price of chicken feed, "Now Abbie, what do you say? I can't sit by any longer and watch you go through all this—" His hand made a sweeping gesture that took in the fallen fence post, the trampled garden, and her dust-streaked person.

A bubble of hysterical laughter escaped Abbie's lips, and Jamie looked aggrieved. "I wish you'd be serious about this," he said.

When Abbie had stifled her first reaction—unbelief and mirth—anger set in. "Thanks!" she said smartly, "but no thanks! When I want a man, Jamie, I'll hire one. That's what you're offering isn't it? A hired man, for free?"

"Now wait a minute! It's not exactly like that—"

"What is it—exactly?"

"You know you need help, Abbie," Jamie said reasonably, "and I'm willing. We could combine our assets—you in the house, where you belong, and me—"

Abbie cut him off with an impatient movement. And with as much dignity as she could muster, she got to her feet. And with a haughtiness only slightly spoiled by her tumbled hair and the dust tracks on her cheeks, she said clearly, "Take back your heart—I ordered liver!"

The silly phrase, heard once in a school play, rose to her lips and hung ridiculously on the air between them as Abbie marched away.

Jamie's mouth fell open. Wordless, he could only gape at her retreating back.

When the kitchen door slammed on Abbie's mocking laugh, Jamie's inflamed reaction to her overwhelming problems subsided rapidly, and a sense of dismay replaced it. What had possessed him?

Groping through his emotions, Jamie attempted to sort them out. The painful progress was interrupted abruptly when a small girl hurled herself into his arms. A wiggling dog leaped and licked his face, and two sweaty boys plopped down beside him, panting and happy, dangling several gopher tails in their grimy hands.

"Hey," one of them said, "where's the pail? And the rope? How are we supposed to get a drink?"

When it became obvious the pail was missing and the rope with it, four heads leaned over the opening to the well, peering into its cool depths. Far below bobbed the pail, the rope tied to it.

Muttering to himself, Jamie set about contriving a pole with a hook on the end and dunked and fished until he managed to pull the lost pail to the surface. Lips tight, he tied the rope securely to the well.

Watching from the window, Abbie was both humiliated and relieved. And when Jamie took tools from the shed and trimmed the end of the broken fence post, setting it back in the ground, firming it with sod and rocks and straightening the twisted wires, the mix of guilt and appreciation increased.

Whistling carelessly, Jamie marched off toward home, without a glance in the direction of the house.

"Jamie said some dumbbell let the rope and pail fall into the well," reported Corky as the children trooped into the house.

"Well, well—," muttered Abbie, and the children laughed uproariously at her feeble attempt at humor.

21

*H*aving just watched her parents drive away in the buggy, headed for Meridian, and with Collum helping a neighbor for the day, the small sound of the screen door's squeak brought Carolyn's head around, and her hands stilled in the soapy pan of water.

"Micah!" Soapy hands and all, she flew to him and clasped him to her, her arms around his neck and her face pressed to his chest.

"I said I'd come back," he said.

"And I said I'd wait." Carolyn tipped her head and looked earnestly up at the dark face above her. Micah's arms had not gone around her and his eyes, unreadable, stared over her head.

"And I'm still waiting. Micah—I need you to tell me—"

"That's why I'm here. You've heard about Cheri."

"I saw her at the picnic—your daughter."

"I brought her from the reservation. You see, I love her—"

"And I love *you*, Micah."

"I hope—enough," Micah said quietly, and with his two hands loosed her arms.

"Enough," Carolyn said sturdily, stepping back and waiting patiently.

"I was very young," Micah said, still in that quiet, determined voice, "and very rebellious. You wouldn't know, but I was wild against my lot here, what I thought of as discrimination."

"But—"

"I know. Wildrose people are good and most of them are kind. But whether real or imagined, I felt different and resented it." Taking a deep breath, he continued, "On the reservation, enjoying freedom for the first time, I did things I'm not proud of now. Among them was a sort of madness for a girl—an older woman, really."

"Cheri's mother."

"Chee, Cheri's mother. Eventually I began to get my wits about me, you might say, and realized my life was, after all, here with my family and among old friends."

"Chee, Micah." Carolyn's voice was steady. "Are you married to Chee?"

"Not as you think of marriage, Caro. Only in the Indian way."

"You mean—you are free?"

"Legally, yes."

A long silence fell; somewhere a meadowlark trilled, somewhere a calf bawled; somewhere, somewhere else, life went on. Here, momentarily, it stood still.

Carolyn caught her breath and, at the sound, the world began its spin once more, and life went on. "I see," she said.

The black eyes turned the full blaze of their despair on her, and Carolyn said strongly, "It doesn't matter, Micah. It doesn't matter."

Only then did Micah's arms reach for her, holding the slim form to him as a drowning man clings to a slim chance of life.

* * *

The currant bushes in the Jameson garden were heavy with ripe fruit. Jamie, in one of the stilted conversations he now had with Abbie when necessary, had offered it to her. Made into sauce or jelly, it would give a welcome change from the limited variety of fruit available from the bush.

Pails in hand, Abbie and the children walked to the Jameson farm. The currant bushes were located at the end of the garden plot, and they went to work.

Straightening her back, Abbie studied Jamie's garden: it was sadly neglected. With the work of two farms to handle as well as household tasks, the garden had been left to develop as it would. It looked as if the beans and peas were drying on the vines, carrots were ready for digging, turnips too.

Abbie set down her pail, admonished the children against eating too many berries, and walked to the house. Inside the open door Jamie was frying something.

Abbie knocked, and Jamie raised startled eyes. "What can I do for you?" he asked shortly as he lifted an iron skillet and set it toward the back of the range, his brown arms rippling under rolled-up shirt sleeves.

What a waste of muscle, Abbie thought fleetingly.

"I just wanted to talk to you," she said.

Probably coming to the conclusion that she wouldn't discuss it from the step, Jamie sighed and said, "Well, come in," and swept a chair clean. Hastily he pushed aside the dishes at Abbie's elbow, shooed off a stubborn fly, and finally threw a dishtowel over the table. Too late he noted Abbie's eyes lingering on the discolored rag.

"Can I offer you something? Tea?" Jamie asked politely, lifting a cracked, brown teapot in his mighty fist as though it were the most elaborate silver service and this, an elegant parlor.

"No thanks," Abbie said, feeling no inclination to trust her health to the dubious cleanliness of the cups hanging in Jamie's open cupboard or her taste buds to the bitter brew he was pouring for himself.

"Well, then!" he said pleasantly and apropos of nothing. Too pleasantly, was Abbie's conclusion; obviously Jamie was smarting under the embarrassment of having her catch him less than proficient at woman's work.

"Jamie," she said mildly, "your vegetables are going to waste out there."

Seating himself opposite her, Jamie shrugged.

"What will you do next winter?" she asked.

"Oh," he said largely, "I'll manage."

"If you mean you won't starve, I suppose you're right." Abbie turned a disdainful eye on the frying pan. "Jamie, what *are* you cooking?"

"I doubt you've heard of it," Jamie said, his eyes fixed on his cup.

Abbie sniffed. "Bacon—onions—"

"Bacon *grease*," Jamie corrected. "Onions, turnips, beans, and—a few more things." With a wicked gleam in his eye, he added, "Care for some?"

Abbie shuddered.

"Well, there's always pork and beans." And Jamie motioned toward a box by the door, overflowing with empty cans.

"Jamie, Jamie, Jamie," Abbie clucked. "What's to become of you?"

Jamie shrugged again.

"You poor, poor thing," Abbie crooned, and immediately Jamie looked wary. And with good reason. Abbie finished with "You need a wife!"

A flush tinged Jamie's brown cheeks.

"Let me offer my services," Abbie continued. "Let me cook for you—and scrub—and wash your clothes. Yes, and mend your trousers." She cast a withered glance at the puckered patch on the knee of Jamie's overalls. "And do your canning, and wash your windows, and weed your garden, and feed your chickens." As though inspired, Abbie was gaining momentum as she went.

Jamie sank lower and lower in his chair. "All right, all right!" he muttered.

"The price of a virtuous woman is far above rubies, Jamie. But, being the pray-er that you are, you have one on order!"

With a flourish only slightly lessened by Worth's old trousers gathered bulkily at the waist and stained with berries, Abbie rose and made her way to the door. "Oh Jamie," she said, turning and sniffing the air delicately, "I think your slum-glullion is burning."

Abbie gathered her brood and marched them down the lane toward home.

And the dreary flies settled unnoticed on the drab dishtowel and the unsavory meal dried in the pan and Jamie stared blindly at the uneven stitches in the patch on the knee of his overalls.

*　*　*

Who can say when summer turns to fall? Perhaps it is in the crisp tang of the early-morning air, the subtle changes in the fragrances—from sunbaked to sunburnt as berries shriveled and grasses browned. Gathered vegetables testified to it, golden grain heavy on its stem confirmed it, gradual diminishing of birdsong corroborated it.

But the opening of school established it. Children forced boots back on feet spread by freedom, gathered up books dusty from disuse, and scuffled through paths that had overgrown with grass that now drooped as surely as their spirits.

At the Runyon brothers' woodpile, Willie's attention was caught by a movement at the top of the hill. A small, brown-clad figure rolled under the fence, got to its feet, and stumbled across the stubbled field, obviously making for the barn and bypassing the house.

The sounds that drifted from the direction of the school indicated that the children were dispersing over the lot for their lunch and an hour of play. Willie knew the procedure. Although there had been no school when his parents settled on their homestead, and Willie was taught at home by his mother, eventually a small log building was erected. At first school was held only during the summer months; farms were few and far between and, in many cases, children were ill-equipped, clothes-wise, for the trudge through bitter snows to a distant school. But when he attended, Willie had played Run Sheep Run with the best of them and tossed a handmade ball in Annie Annie Over as happily as the next child. That Simon was not now engaged in such pleasure spelled trouble.

Thoughtfully Willie laid aside the axe and turned his lanky frame in the direction of the barn into which the small figure had disappeared. Hesitating at the door, a rustle overhead broke the silence, and Willie strode to the ladder on the wall and began to climb. As his head cleared the opening he saw the boy in a corner of the mow, sitting crosslegged on a mound of hay and looking fixedly at a piece of straw in his hand.

Willie clambered up, crossed the dusty floor, and lowered himself to the boy's side.

"I'm not goin' back!" Attempting belligerence, the voice merely quavered.

"Well, now," said Willie, putting a straw in the corner of his mouth, "that's not too unusual. I remember a day when I didn't go at all."

Simon turned round eyes on the cadaverous face. "You?"

"Sure. Lots of kids do it, one time or another."

"But I'm *never* goin' back."

"Hmmmm. Care to talk about it?"

"No!" The boy was emphatic.

Willie settled back on one elbow, long legs stretched before him, ankles crossed, and chewed thoughtfully on the straw.

Simon fiddled nervously with the straw in his hand. "I hate it!" he cried vehemently.

"Mr. Fairchild probably is a mean teacher."

"Not him. He's nice."

"It's no fun, learning to read and write and all that."

Simon hesitated. "That's all right, I guess."

"Dumb bunch of kids."

"Most of them're nice."

"Hmmmm . . ."

"All except one. And he says—he says—" Simon gulped. "He says bad things, and I hate him, and I won't go back!"

"I know what you mean," Willie said sympathetically.

"You know?" breathed the boy.

"Sure. When I was a kid, in that same school, one fella said awful things. I wanted to punch his face, but, you see, he was bigger'n me."

Simon's nodding head shone in a ray of sunshine.

"He kept calling me 'ugly duckling.' Wouldn't stop. Just kept sayin' it."

"You ain't ugly!"

"Truth of the matter is, he was right. I *was* ugly. But I couldn't help it, could I? And I had to live with it, didn't I?"

Simon was looking uncertain.

"I finally decided there were other things about me that were good, as good as anybody else—maybe better. I was good at sports, I was good-natured, I had a good home, and a mother who loved me, ugly or not. I really enjoyed life—except for that boy. I decided I wasn't going to let him spoil everything for me. So I just ignored him. Pretty soon he quit."

Simon was thinking seriously. "He says—," he hesitated, "he teases me because I don't have a father."

"Shoot!" said Willie grandly. "Neither do I. Haven't had one since I can remember, almost! Do you think that's going to ruin my life? No sirree. I've got good friends, like Hubert and Harry, and now I've got you."

Simon studied the craggy face with its deep, kind eyes. "I think I'll go back now," he said, "before the bell rings."

"I would if I were you."

The man and boy left the barn together. Willie watched as Simon trotted across the field, rolled under the fence, turned and waved, and disappeared. When he turned toward the woodpile again, Willie saw Sarah in the doorway of the house.

Between swings, Willie heard the screen door slam and light steps approach. "Simon," Sarah said hesitantly, "what was troubling him?"

"Just havin' a bad day," Willie answered casually, leaning on the axe.

Sarah sat down on the chopping block; the eyes she raised to the man towering over her were vulnerable. Abruptly, he set the axe aside, sat down, and put his huge hands on his knees. He looked at the woman with steady eyes.

Her gaze was just as steady, and so was her voice when she said, "Willie—I wasn't married to Simon's father. You knew that, of course."

When Willie made a gesture as though to interrupt, she said, "No, let me go on. I want you to know.

"I was just a kid when my mother died. My father, probably heartbroken, wandered off somewhere for a while. But before he left, he hired me out to a farm where the woman was bedridden. I worked like a—a beast of burden, I guess you could say.

"The farm was isolated, there was no one else there—just a sick woman, a cruel, abusive man, and me. There was no other place for me." Sarah's fine face showed signs of strain, and her gray eyes were haunted as with memories too terrible to remember, too terrible to forget.

"I don't think you need to go on," Willie said gently.

Sarah's head bowed over her tightly clasped hands, and she whispered, wonderingly, "You understand, don't you? You understand!"

"I'd be a fool not to," Willie said gruffly.

"Eventually," Sarah continued in a muffled voice, "my grandmother found me and took me to live with her.

"When a girl's reputation is smirched, people aren't the same toward you. And men—men seem to take for granted—" Sarah's voice revealed her desperate misery. "It was worse, though, for Simon than for me, especially when he went to school. He was—is—innocent. So innocent. And how can I explain to him that he's a child of . . . ?"

A tear, fat and shining, fell from the tip of Sarah's nose, followed by others in fast succession, until the front of her waist was spotted with the evidence of her pain and humiliation.

"Passed away," Willie said, and repeated it strongly: "Passed away!"

Sarah looked up, startled. "Passed away?"

"In Christ," Willie said. "Old things pass away; behold, all things become new."

Unwinding his long legs, Willie stretched his lanky body, reached for the axe, and returned to the woodpile.

The gray eyes that followed him, usually the only indication of the woman's feelings, were luminous as she whispered, "Behold . . ."

22

*J*amie," Abbie said when Jamie came to rake the hay he had mowed previously, "is there anything I can get you from the store?"

"Today?"

"This afternoon."

"I thought Sam and Regina were helping the Blums with their threshing today."

"They are."

"Well," Jamie appeared to be puzzled, "who's going?"

"I'm going, just like I said," Abbie explained with elaborate patience.

"You're surely not thinking of walking. Wait a day or so and I'll be going; you and the children can ride along."

"I have a perfectly good buggy in the shed, Jamie, and as you're using your own horses today, I'll take Beauty."

Jamie almost dropped the traces he was fastening. "You've never used the buggy," he said curtly. "Wait until I have time, and I'll—"

"Nonsense! I'm perfectly capable, and it all seems perfectly simple. And I have to start sometime. It will be a—an adventure for the children and me."

Abbie didn't try to put into words the sense of isolation that pinched her soul and withered her gregarious spirit. Although she was busy past thinking most of the time, there were moments when the four log walls of the house and the hardly larger walls of the surrounding bush seemed like prison walls. Her dependence on Jamie and Sam for transportation was becoming more and more galling—and if for her, perhaps much more so for them. Yes, it was time to take another step along the path toward independence.

But behind the brave front she presented to Jamie lurked considerable uneasiness; the project didn't seem "perfectly simple" at all. Among several anxieties, two were more fearsome than the others, and they dealt with each end of the horse: How to put on the breeching equipment, which meant inserting the tail through the crupper, and second, getting the bit in the horse's mouth. In wild dreams the last few nights, Beauty, resenting the crupper (as well she might, thought a sympathetic Abbie), trod all over Abbie's feet. And as for the bit, Beauty refused it, tossing her head forever out of Abbie's reach. From each nightmare Abbie had awakened in a cold sweat.

Collar, harness pad, gig saddle, hame straps, breast strap, traces! Abbie tried to sort them all out and made several efforts to be in the barnyard when Jamie was hitching or unhitching, surreptitiously watching which buckle went where, how each piece of harness fit, and how it was hitched to the rig. (And was there really a *whiffletree?* And if so, where? Abbie was inclined to think it was a monstrous joke on Jamie's part.)

When the harness was not on the horse, but hanging on a nail in the barn, it was simply a confusing tangle of leather straps, loops, and buckles, and Abbie's heart shuddered.

I'm going to do it today, she insisted stubbornly, and watched Jamie one more time. He went about the task of hitching the team to the hay rake, tight-lipped, grim-faced, stiff-shouldered. Poor Jamie, she thought, half amused at his mutterings and half vexed at his black brow. I really am a trial to him. But so is he to me!

"Good luck!" Jamie managed tightly as he heaved himself into the rake's seat. Growling a "Giddup!" to the team, he rattled across the barnyard toward the opening in the bush and the meadow beyond, the rake's 20 steel teeth glinting in the morning sun.

With a shake of her shoulders, Abbie turned to the children. "All right," she said smartly, "get your jobs done! We're going to town this afternoon!"

After excited exclamations and a few happy jig steps, Corcoran and Cameron went to the garden to strip the vines of their final crop, and Merry set about gathering eggs.

It was early afternoon when Abbie called the boys—who were loud in their declaration that they could do it all by themselves—to come and help her, and they made their way to the barn and the uncertain task before them.

When the door creaked open and the sun's rays fell across the floor, lighting up the dim interior and the horse in her stall, all three stopped in their tracks, open-mouthed. Beauty was fully harnessed.

The boys cried out in surprise, wondering if elves had been at work; at times Abbie heartily regretted reading so many fairy tales to them. But with a lump in her throat, she conceded that some good elf had indeed done them a good deed. Then, limp with relief, she led Beauty over the sill and into the yard.

The hitching-up was tense, especially the backing. But the horse knew what she was doing even if the woman didn't, and the boys maneuvered the shafts so that the connection was made satisfactorily. With every buckle fastened (to something or other!), Abbie led the horse to the house, and she and the children went to get ready.

With Corcoran, Cameron, and Merry dressed and waiting impatiently on the step with orders to stay clean, Abbie bathed herself, put on a changeable silk waist with puff-top sleeves and a handsome choker collar, and a black-figured moiré skirt, "rustle" lined, interlined with canvas at the bottom and with a full four-yard sweep.

Piling her tawny hair in a heap on the top of her head, she fastened a modest straw turban—trimmed with three quills and rosettes of ribbon and knots of velvet—on her head. Her mirrored smile changed to a frown when she leaned forward to study the few freckles spilled across the bridge of her nose; they faded, but failed to disappear, under a discreet application of Fleur de Lis powder. Sighing, she touched the glass stopper of Lily of the Valley toilet water behind each ear, picked up the walrus-grain leather bag she had purchased on her honeymoon, and turned to go.

But first, add wood to the range and thrust the chicken into the oven. If they were to eat tonight, plans had to be made. Like Cinderella at the ball, Abbie thought ruefully as she closed the door and stepped up into her well-sprung carriage with its genuine machine-buffed leather seat, velvet carpet, and elegant gold stripe, the moment would come when her fancy clothes must be laid aside and harsh responsibilities resumed.

But Cinderella had a handsome prince waiting in the wings. Abbie shook her head and admitted she was getting as fanciful as the boys. Happily ever after indeed!—fairy stories.

At the last moment, Abbie cast a swift look around and found herself disappointed that Jamie, who had called her "half man, half woman," was nowhere in sight.

Flapping the reins professionally on Beauty's broad back, Abbie cried "Giddup!" in a fair imitation of Jamie's earlier command and, to her relief, the horse started off obediently. A slight pull on the rein and she turned toward Meridian, and Abbie's confidence grew.

Catching the children's obvious enjoyment, Abbie let the cares of the past months slip from her shoulders. Contentment—uninvited but unrefused—crept out of the shadows of her heart into the light. "Count your many blessings; see what God hath done," she hummed, and soon sang aloud, the children joining in.

At "name them one by one," Corcoran pointed to a meadowlark on a fence post and shouted, "Birds!" And truly, glorious song poured from bush and meadow, as though the feathered creatures were storing up a plethora of happy sound against the silent months just ahead when they would be gone.

"The sky!" warbled Merry, catching the spirit of the game. And the magnificent sky, like a great blue coverlet tufted with cotton-batting clouds, stretched endlessly overhead.

"Fragrance!" breathed Abbie, and they all breathed deeply of the aroma that was peculiar to the bush; just now it was a potpourri of withering berries, mown grass, damp leafmold, and fading flowers.

"Food!" shouted an always-hungry Cameron, and Abbie gave a grateful thought to the chicken roasting in the oven, and the stocked shelves in the cellar after a summer of the bush's abundance.

"Friends!"

Abbie's sense of gratitude grew as she gave thanks for the good people of Wildrose and their strength and support—Brother Victor, Sam and Regina, Jamie. In particular—Jamie. Again that lump rose in Abbie's throat as she thought of Jamie as, unasked and unthanked, he had harnessed the horse for a woman he knew was dreading the job, was probably incapable of doing it, and too proud to admit it.

They broke free of the bush, crossed the railroad track, and tied up at the general store hitching rail. The one stop did it all; post office and store were under one roof. Holding the hem of her skirt out of the dust (all four yards of it!), Abbie followed the scampering children into the crowded interior. Everything a homesteader might need was here—everything a homemaker might want, not always so. Abbie gave thanks for the items stored in her shed and dreaded the day the children should outgrow the shoes she still unpacked from time to time.

Now she purchased the few necessities she needed—sugar for canning, rubber rings for last year's jars, vinegar and spices for pickling, a few crackers from the open barrel to nibble on the trip home.

Proudly packaged on the counter were a few loaves of bread, an experiment by a baker in Prince Albert, shipped out once a week by train. Adding one to her purchases as a special treat, Abbie impulsively included a second loaf, a small thank-you to a man who hated baking bread and who existed, according to his own word, almost entirely on "fried potatoes and pork and beans."

She tucked two letters from "home" into her bag, savoring the pleasure they would bring when she was quiet and alone, and inquired about Jamie's mail. With a lone advertisement for the "Celebrated Sherwin Patent Adjustable Field Roller" in her hand, Abbie's heart went out to the lonely neighbor, and she added another blessing to her list: "Thank You, Heavenly Father, for my children!"

Those three blessings were soon clamoring for pennies, and spent enthralled minutes before the candy counter. Then, with lemon drops clutched in already sticky fingers, they followed their mother to the rig to begin a more subdued but equally happy trip back home.

Corcoran roused himself to reach for a cracker and called out in alarm, "Mum! Look!" His finger pointed to a buggy wheel, tipping as it turned, and making crazy patterns in the dust of the road.

"Whoa!" Abbie pulled up on the lines. The wheel, stopping, rested at a slant, leaning at the top away from the buggy.

Beauty stood patiently while Abbie and the children piled out and studied the situation. "It's broke," Corcoran pronounced.

"Something's wrong, that's for sure."

"Haywire," Cameron said wisely.

"We can't leave it here in the middle of the road," Abbie said, and stepped to Beauty's head, put a hand on the bridle and urged her a slow step by step ahead until, the wheel reeling ever more wildly, the buggy rested at the side of the narrow roadway.

"We'll have to leave the buggy and hoof it," Abbie said, and the children bent in gales of laughter.

"Hoof it! We ain't—haven't—got hoofs!"

But their hilarity faded before they had walked very far. Abbie led Beauty, and Merry, small legs astraddle, rode; it was all Abbie could do to hoist her that high. The boys trudged along manfully after Abbie had made an abortive attempt to give them a "leg up." For her efforts she was left with a dusty moiré skirt and a tipped straw turban.

Realizing Beauty didn't need leading, Abbie gave both hands to the canvas sack she had been loath to leave behind in the buggy. The twins each carried a bag, and Merry clutched two loaves of bakery bread.

"How far is it, Mama?" Merry asked.

"Not far, dear," Abbie said in as comforting a tone as she could command, seeing that her "Fine Coin-toe Shoe," cut from "the very finest Vici Kid stock, with hand-turned soles, newest fancy heel foxing, patent leather tips, and tops faced with the very best of black silk," were cruelly pinching her toes—and that in spite of the fact that the "coin" feature, guaranteed to be the very newest style worn in the large cities (and Abbie in the backwoods!), was also called the "quarter toe," being about the width of a 25-cent piece.

"These things are a hazard," Abbie now concluded grimly, as the narrow toes peeked turnabout from under the draggled hem of her skirt. "I could stave off attacking coyotes with them!"

"It is too, far!" corrected Cameron. "We haven't even come to Miko's house."

"The Vashinskis! We can't be far from their place."

Burdened, dusty, limping, hat askew, and sack dragging, Abbie's hopes lifted and she urged the tiring children on with promises of help at the Vashinski homestead. Then, coming at a trot over the brow of a small hill, a buggy and horse came into view.

"Jamie!" shrieked the children. And it was.

Jamie had come in from the meadow late in the afternoon to find the buggy gone from the shed. Heading for home, he expected to meet the little family at any moment. From his barn, and then from his house, he watched and listened, and his uneasiness for Abbie and the children grew. Finally, as the sun began its slide toward the horizon, he hitched a horse to his buggy and headed out.

A bedraggled sight met his eyes: Abbie—weighted with her burden, limping badly, her finery soiled, and her hair tumbling under a tipping hat—led a small parade: one plodding horse with its small rider and two tired boys straining at the sacks in their sweaty hands.

The little band stood to the side of the road, the twins waving and cheering loudly as Jamie approached. Abbie's smile was tremulous.

Jamie pulled to a halt and studied them, and compassion for the brave woman may have shown in his eyes, for

Abbie, rather than tilting her chin and giving him stare for stare, smiled timidly and said, "I might have known it."

Jamie climbed out of the buggy and helped Abbie and the boys into the rig, lifted Merry from Beauty's back, crushing beyond repair the bread she hugged, set her on her mother's lap, and tied Beauty behind the buggy. The chattering boys filled him in on the crippled buggy they had left at the side of the road.

"I'll come back for it," Jamie said. I knew better than to let them go without checking that buggy over, he told himself grimly, blaming himself.

But Abbie was saying, "I should have listened to you . . ."

A humbled Abbie was not something Jamie was sure he appreciated after all. "There was no way you could know the wheel needed attention," he said, and turned the rig and headed for home.

When a weary Abbie and her children climbed down from Jamie's buggy in their own yard, Abbie took one of the crumpled packages from Merry's arms. "For you, Jamie. I'm sorry it's in such a wretched shape."

Jamie took the mashed bread and said, as a crown prince might when offered the crown of the realm, "I'm proud to have it."

23

*I*n a small log house, privacy is hard to come by—and especially so when the weather is bad and family members are housebound.

With the first threat of winter and a chill in the air, with the last garden produce stored away in the cellar and no more fruit to can, with the house sweetened and spotless, awaiting the onslaught of another winter's soot and sweat and smells, women, particularly, were shut into their whitewashed prison as surely as though iron bars had closed around them.

In the Morris home, roomier than many—two rooms up and two down—Carolyn found herself desperately in need of a time to be alone and a place where she could think and pray without interruption—or worse yet, without questioning glances and troubled looks.

"It doesn't matter," she had said quickly to Micah. "It doesn't matter," she had said, without thought and without prayer. Now she wondered. Now she felt the unrest of a troubled spirit, new to her in her innocence, but clearly recognized nevertheless. The week's laundry dulled it for a time. It subsided during the supper hour when conversation blossomed. The occasional visitor brought enough interest to cancel it out momentarily.

But given a moment to herself, she found the inner uneasiness pushed itself from the subconscious to the conscious level and insisted on attention.

While she scattered feed to the chickens, her mind wrestled with the situation: Micah married and yet not married. With her hands in dishwater, her thoughts swung from the certainty of Micah's love for her to his responsibility to the Indian woman Chee. Heaving a four-pound iron around on bunglesome garments, she persisted in her disclaimer, "It doesn't matter," and despaired at the turmoil in her spirit that gave her words the lie.

Having led nothing but a "quiet and peaceable life in all godliness and honesty," and with a conscience that had never been riffled except over a "small" lie or a childish deceit, she was at a loss to understand or cope with the strong surges that troubled her now. When, in desperation, she sought insight into her agitation from the Bible, she equated the Psalmist's ferment of spirit with her own when he said, "All thy waves and thy billows are gone over me." But she was no nearer a solution.

And this unusual concentration on God's Word was a betrayal of her problem. Her mother's eyebrows lifted and she studied Carolyn's face earnestly, obviously suspicious that not all was well.

Nor was there any help from Brother Victor's Sunday sermon on the scripture, "The harvest is past, the summer is ended, and we are not saved." Although Arnie Dudley, convicted of a summer of wild abandon and anticipating a winter with a guilty conscience, made his penitent way to the mourner's bench, Carolyn knew sin was not her problem.

But when, the following Sunday, the preacher quoted, "Peace, peace; when there is no peace," Carolyn's heart tuned in. Here, at last, was the problem in a nutshell: There was no peace. And having wrestled for too long with its alternative—a troubled mind and an uneasy spirit—she knew she could settle for no less than peace, perfect peace.

"Perhaps the answer," Pastor Victor offered, "is found in the apostle's advice to the Romans: 'Follow after the things which make for peace.'

"If we have 'sown the wind,'" he said, "we shall 'reap the whirlwind.' The 'effect of righteousness,' on the other hand, is 'quietness and assurance.'" And how Carolyn's poor, battered heart needed that!

The Savior came, he explained, to "guide our feet into the way of peace." Self-will seeks its own way and finds it rough going; a submissive spirit seeks God's way and finds it a way of peace.

It was a thoughtful Carolyn who made her way out of the schoolhouse/church, through dinner and supper, and to bed. There, in the only privacy possible to her aside from an unexplainable walk through the afternoon's drenching rain, she relinquished her own way and her own plans for those of a higher and wiser power. Not knowing the future but knowing One who did, she turned over and went to sleep understanding, at last, the verse learned routinely in Sunday School sometime across the years: "The Lord will give strength unto his people; the Lord will bless his people with peace." It was all the strength she needed; it was the necessary peace.

If, in the morning, the pillowcase was tearstained, no one knew it but the weary—but peaceful—young woman who made up the bed and recognized it as her Bethel— Bethel, where Jacob of old took stones, "put them for his pillows, and lay down in that place to sleep," and heard from God.

The hand that wrote the note—to be slipped to Tiger Lille at the Wednesday night prayer meeting—was steady.

24

*P*eering through their prized spectacles, Hubert and Harry clutched the porch posts and strained for a glimpse of the binder. When the vagrant breeze turned momentarily in their direction, withered nostrils quivered and shrunken chests filled with remembered scents of harvest, and they fancied they could catch the sound of the machine's familiar clack. But the tangle of pin cherry, saskatoon, and chokecherry bushes that circled the field hid the man and the harvester except for the brief tantalizing second when they topped a small rise, to disappear again.

Hubert's feet shuffled.

"Don't even think about it!" Harry warned.

"Ah, Harry, c'mon! It ain't all that far."

"You poor thing," Harry said pityingly. "You must be wearin' magnifying glasses—that field is a quarter of a mile off. And you know it, if your rememberer ain't as bent out of shape as your eyeballs!"

"Not when he turns at this end," Hubert argued. "If we start out now, we could get there by the time he makes two, three more turns."

Harry's fierce expression faded and his eyes filled with longing.

"It may be our last chance," Hubert urged.

Harry's sigh admitted it.

"We could take Willie his midmorning snack. Poor feller—must be gettin' pretty hungry. Been at it since dawn, almost."

"You gonna carry it?"

"I only need one hand for a cane, Harry. And how heavy can a biscuit and a dab o' jam be?"

When Harry threw up his hands in capitulation, Hubert turned to the door, open to one of the last warm days of the year, and called, "Sarah, Harry'n me'll take Willie's sandwich to him."

Quick, light steps brought Sarah to the doorway; her strong face softened at the sight of the old chin lifted challengingly toward her. Hubert's bluster faded, and he added, with a plea in his tone for understanding, "And it will save you a trip."

"I'll get it ready," Sarah said.

"See," Hubert said brightly, turning to his brother. "She thinks it's a good idea."

"You poor thing," Harry said again. "You're sure lungin' at your tether today. I'll have to go along with you just to be sure you make it. Hey!" he cried in alarm. "Don't sit down! You'll be so long gettin' up, we'll have to take supper to him."

But Hubert made a creaking descent to the porch's one step, lowered himself, and set about tying the bootlaces that dangled around his feet. "Stick your foot over here," he said when he had finished, "and I'll do yourn."

Supposing it was easier, after all, than getting up and down, Harry clung to the post and extended one foot, and then the other. "Easy now," he admonished. "Not too tight, or you'll cut off my circulation."

"Your blood's so tired it won't make it to your kneecaps until tomorrow."

Sarah's appearance put an end to the repartee, the best the brothers had come up with for days. She straightened the buttons on Hubert's ancient knitted cardigan, handed them their shapeless caps, and suggested casually, "Why don't you let Simon go too? He spends so much time alone."

"Good idea!" Hubert said heartily. "We can tell him about when we grubbed that field—and how we harvested our first crop with a scythe. It wasn't so easy in the old days, you know."

Sarah called, and Simon tumbled from a poplar tree and came running.

"The uncles have some interesting things to tell you about the good old days."

"Aw—" Simon's face fell. "I heard all about those before."

"Did I tell you about the bear that was pickin' saskatoons right over there?" Hubert said. "And how it made Virgie so mad to have him stealin' her berries she hollered 'Shoo!' at him?"

"Honest?" breathed the boy, and the small face lit up. He automatically took the lunch pail his mother handed him and lent his shoulder to the elderly man who made his laborious way off the porch, followed by his brother.

"That bear story," Harry said with a sniff, "ain't nothin' compared to the one about the time I cut my leg bad with the scythe and had to limp clear across the pasture with the bull sniffin' the wind, pawin' the ground, and workin' his way closer and closer—"

"There's enough food for all of you," Sarah called after the trio as they made their way across the yard, the small boy's face lifted with fascination from one to the other of the talkative old men.

With a smile, Sarah settled down on the step, leaned back, closed her eyes, and breathed deeply. Almost she wished she had accompanied the uncles and the boy; the crisp fall air, redolent with dried berries, fresh-cut hay and grain, and the summer's last burst of flowers, called for an outing, a walk through the browning grasses of the meadows and falling leaves of the bush.

Harvest was the culmination of the year's work. All across the bush and the stretching prairies to the south, a sense of urgency prodded the farmer to dawn-to-dark effort to bring in the crop. When it was safely garnered in, the grim face of winter receded a little, outstanding bills were paid, a few necessities purchased, and—with the year's work largely completed—social gatherings enjoyed, at least for that brief and blessed period between frenetic summer and fall and the enforced idleness of winter.

This year, winter with its isolation held no terrors for Sarah. Rather, the seclusion of the tight log house with its warm fires, full cellar, and gentle companions beckoned the young woman with its promise of peace and security. The dark years were behind her at last. Here, in this backwoods asylum, she had found contentment. Here, she felt, she was willing to spend the rest of her life—her lonely life.

For in spite of the uncles' garrulousness, a certain emptiness marked Sarah's days. In spite of an active child's chatter, a quiet loneliness existed.

But it was so much better than she had known, so free of anguish, so healing in its silent promise of a better day, that she wrapped herself in her small, sure blessings and counted herself happy.

Come spring, she thought now, she would start a chicken yard of her own. And why not their own cow? Perhaps, if a part of their grain and hay could be stored, a horse . . .

Sarah's thoughts were interrupted by the sound of an approaching rig turning in at the gate. Automatically put-

ting a hand to her head to straighten her hair and standing
to her feet and shaking out her skirts, she studied the horse
and buggy and the lone man in it.

Except for church attendance, a few trips to Meridian,
and calls by two or three Wildrose ladies, Sarah's summer
had been spent on her uncles' homestead. No rig—other
than Willie's and the preacher's—was known to her by
sight. Consequently, she watched curiously as the horse
trotted smartly toward her.

Stepping from the porch's shelter with a ready smile,
Sarah's "Good morning" died in her throat on a strangled
croak, and a horror of disbelief washed over her. It
couldn't be—

But it was.

Fondling the buggy whip (that might have been my
first clue, she thought irrationally, for who in Wildrose
used a whip on the family transportation?), the man
pushed his hat off his forehead, looked her over from slit-
ted eyes beneath bushy brows, and through lips whose
loose fullness was all too sickeningly known to the watching woman, said, "It's been a while."

Sarah's hand went to her throat.

With a grunt, the man heaved himself from the rig. "Is
that the best you can do?" he said. "After all this time?
How long has it been, Sarie?"

Still Sarah said nothing, could say nothing.

"Well, how old's the boy?" he asked impatiently.
"Didn't think I knew about him, did you?"

"I . . . I . . ."

"Just as speechless as ever, I see," the man said. "I
thought growing up might have helped. Let's see—how
old were you? A child, Sarie—an innocent child . . ."

Sarah's pale face went paler still.

"Seven years, Sarie. Seven years since you skipped
out. Left me alone with a sick wife. And all that work. But

never mind." The voice turned hearty. "Here you are, all grown up."

"What do you want?" Finding her voice at last, Sarah's tone was desperate.

"Why you, of course," the man said with lifted eyebrow, smiling now—smiling—leering.

"Mamie's dead, you see. Do you understand what that means?"

Sarah looked blank.

"It means we can get married." The fleshy face pressed close to hers, the voice lowered: "None of the hired girls after you were as good as you, Sarie—"

Backing from the large figure, Sarah found her voice at last. "Get out of here! Get out, I say!" The last found her tone escalating with a touch of panic she had hoped never to feel again.

"Remember this, Sarie?" the man said softly, flourishing the whip. "Don't make me use it—again."

With a whoosh the man's breath was knocked from him as a small ball of fury launched itself into his stomach. Simon, having turned to see who the arrival might be, had heard his mother's desperate cry. Behind him, legs atremble but coming with a vigor borne of their outrage, Hubert and Harry tottered into the arena of battle.

"Leave my mother alone!" Simon, red-faced and furious, backed off, but his small fists were bunched at his side.

"Ho ho—so this is young Meyer! Quite a pup!"

"My name is Simon," the boy said, scowling. Sarah moved to his side and put her arm around him. Shaking like a poplar leaf in the wind, she said, beseechingly, "Please, Mr. Dieter, leave us alone! Please—please go!"

"Not without you and the boy. You can come willingly," Meyer Dieter said in a hard voice, "or—"

Sarah's reply was a moan of terrible despair.

At the anguish in their niece's voice, Harry and Hubert—until now fixed by astonishment and dismay—exploded into what was, for them, a burst of action.

"Now you—whoever you are—get out of here!" Harry shrilled, starting forward with a menacing gesture of his cane.

"C'mon, Harry," Hubert gritted, "let's show Mister Big Nose who's boss!" And the brothers, canes aloft in a threatening manner, closed in on the contemptuous-faced stranger.

The whip, in the long run, was "boss." One swift snap and Harry and Hubert were cocooned in its leather grip. One hard pull, and they tumbled to the ground.

"Uncles!" Sarah gasped, and flung herself on her knees beside them. She fumbled futilely at the taut binding; Harry and Hubert scrabbled feebly in the dust.

"No—oh, no—oh, no. Darlings, lie still while I—" Sarah's sobs mingled with Hubert's and Harry's groans and Simon's screams. In the general hue and cry Sarah missed the desperation in the sounds emanating from the child until, from the corner of her eye, she caught sight of small legs threshing wildly in midair.

In the process of wiping blood from Hubert's cheek where it had struck a rock when he fell, she turned fully to see Simon struggling helplessly in the bearlike grip of the burly man. Her frenzied effort to jump to her feet entangled her legs in her skirts, and she sprawled awkwardly in the dirt beside her trussed uncles.

With the boy pinioned under his arm, Meyer Dieter was mounting the iron step into the buggy.

"The horse, Sarah!" Harry croaked.

Up and running at last, Sarah well knew the man's strength was not to be coped with and, hearing Harry, she veered toward the horse's head and reached for the bridle.

The man's roared "Giddap!" and his vicious yank on the reins, alternated by urgent slaps to its quivering flanks, startled the horse. Eyes rolling, it jumped and reared, its head tossed beyond Sarah's grasp.

With his big thigh pinning the small boy into the corner of the buggy seat and his two hands free, Meyer Dieter lashed at the horse with the ends of the reins, hauled the alarmed animal around, and curveted across the yard.

Simon's screams were the last thing Sarah heard. As quickly as it had begun, it was over. The sun shone, somewhere a bird trilled, and except for a faint, distant clack, silence reigned. The meaning of the distant sound slowly, foggily, took on meaning—Willie.

The uncles thought of it at the same time.

"Willie!" Harry said, spitting dirt.

"Quick, Sarah!" urged a pale Hubert. "Go get Willie!"

About to turn and run, Sarah hesitated, her eyes on the fallen men.

"Don't worry about us!" Harry said quickly. "I've got my knife in my pocket—"

"Or we'll just roll ourselves out of this mess," Hubert said, and suited action to words by lifting his head, studying the thong around his middle, and advising his brother, "Now if you'll just gee while I haw—"

"Tell Willie it was Rudy's horse!" Harry spluttered as Hubert began his roll. Sarah gathered up her skirts and ran.

Willie, possibly anticipating the arrival of his midmorning repast, had stopped the binder at the point nearest the house and was sauntering toward the fence. Sarah's mindless stumble spoke for itself; he broke into a run to meet her. Long before he reached her he could see her anguished face and hear her words: "He's got Simon—he's got Simon—"

Catching the staggering figure in his arms, Willie spoke sharply, "Who, Sarah? Who has Simon?"

"Dieter—Meyer Dieter."

The name meant nothing to Willie, but he knew instantly.

"Tell me—"

Between heaving sobs and gasps for breath, Sarah explained what had happened. "I don't know where he's taken him," she finished brokenly. "But Harry said it was Rudy's horse and rig."

Rudy was the stationmaster at the Meridian depot.

"He's heading for Meridian, then," Willie said, setting Sarah on her feet and sprinting on long legs to the binder. With practiced fingers, he unhitched and unharnessed, throwing the harness to the ground, except for bridles.

"Take Min to the house," he said, and swung himself up on the back of the younger, lighter horse. With a sharp jab in the surprised mare's side, he guided her—not toward the road, but across the stubbled field.

Sarah watched the clods fly from the horse's feet and saw the man's lean figure bent low over the streaming mane until man and horse disappeared beyond the field, into the silence of the bush, and thence, she knew, to the pasture beyond. From there—

"He's headin' him off at the pass," Hubert offered when Sarah and Min reached the house. Harry, sitting on the step and running a shaky hand through his tousled hair, nodded.

"He'll come out at Dwyer's place, of course. Herb is probably in the field. They'll go on to pick up Shane O'Hara."

"Willie knows every farm in Wildrose as well as he knows his own," Hubert continued. "He's threshed 'em all. And he knows every shortcut between here and Meridian. He'll pick up quite a crew along the way. And they may do some thrashin' before it's all over!" Hubert winked with an eye that was swelling grotesquely in his grim face.

Sarah seemed pathetically crumpled and shrunken. Hubert and Harry looked at each other meaningfully.

"Come over here, dearie," Harry said, tapping the step beside him. "We got more help goin' for us than you may think."

Sarah crept to her uncles, dropped to a seat between them, and put her head in her hands. Harry and Hubert draped protective arms around her shoulders—never mind that they were frail, still shaking from the ordeal they had been through; they were as oaks in their comforting strength—and they bowed their heads.

"You think you kin get it right this time?" Hubert asked.

"I think I kin."

One voice and three hearts lifted in a simple but passionate plea: *Heavenly Father, bring our boy home to us.*

25

The shadows were lengthening when Simon's pup bolted from the kitchen, scrabbled across the rough boards of the porch, and streaked toward the distant horse and weary riders coming down the road. The tall form of the man was bent over the drooping figure of the child. Simon, half asleep, was cradled against Willie's heart.

The dog's shrill barks brought the tired horse's head up and roused the boy. When Sarah's fleet legs followed on the pup's heels and her hungry arms reached, Simon slid from one pair of arms to another. Sarah rocked the child in a transport of joy and relief. Simon went, eventually, from the ecstacy of the mother to the deliriousness of the dog and, finally, to the wordless hugs and pats of the wet-eyed old men who had followed at what was, for them, top speed.

Sarah turned from Simon to Willie as he dismounted. Wrapping her arms around his waist and burying her face in his shirt front, she whispered, "Will. Oh, Will."

Willie's shaggy head went up; his deep-set eyes stared over the woman's head with startled incredulity.

Across all the years of his life it had been Willie. It was Wee Willie Winkie—Willie-nilly—Stringbean Willie during his growing-up years; with adulthood it had changed to

Aw, Willie——C'mon, Willie—Puh-lease, Willie—Hey, Willie. Willie will do it, ask Willie, call on Willie, good ol' Willie were bywords in the community. Even, occasionally, "What would we ever do without Willie?" was heard, or "Willie's an answer to prayer."

No one, in well over 30 years, had afforded him the dignity of Will.

Gently, ever so gently, Willie wrapped his long arms around the young woman pressed against him and laid his gaunt cheek momentarily on her head. Then he released her and walked with her toward the house.

With a tired Simon tucked at last into bed, Sarah joined the uncles at the heater for a cup of tea. Willie had collected the discarded harness and the horse Min and had wended his weary way homeward; evening chores would not be denied, no matter how tired a man might be.

"I can just see it," Hubert exulted for the tenth time. "Willie and Herb and Shane and Dowell—"

"And Curtis and Collum—"

"And Jamie and—"

"The whole passel of 'em! All waitin' at the depot when Mr. Whipenpoof drove in."

Sarah summoned a wan smile, followed by a shiver.

"Don't you worry, dearie," Harry said. "That rapscallion won't dare show his beak anywhere in the bush ever again!"

"Dowell was pitchin' hay when Willie came by," Hubert said for the tenth time, "and he just took the pitchfork along with him. Gordy took that snarlin' dog of his, and Sam grabbed up the hammer from his forge. Man! I'da loved to see that!"

"Somebody had a grub hoe," Harry continued with glee, "and somebody had a manure hook! Jamie had his Winchester, and a coupla guys had shotguns. Even Rudy grabbed up that famous Belgian back-action gun of his!"

"Willie never said in so many words what he told that beefy kidnapper, but the whole kit and kaboodle hustled him onto the train, some of them shakin' their weapons and darin' him to come back."

Willie Tucker, it seemed, had called in his IOUs. Like a Pied Piper he had crossed Wildrose, and without question and without hesitation the men of the district—a score and more—had dropped their work to follow.

"And all for Simon—and me," Sarah said softly.

"That's bush people for you," Hubert said stoutly. "Before you're here very long, you'll have opportunity to pay them back—somebody'll be born or be sick or die, and you'll do what you can." Hu spoke with conviction.

"Thank God for Will," Sarah said with feeling.

Harry and Hubert exchanged puzzled glances. "Will?"

"Without him I wouldn't have Simon tonight. Yes, thank God for Will."

"Thank God," two voices chorused weakly in agreement, "for Will."

*   *   *

On her way to the designated trysting place, Carolyn caught a glimpse of the weary horse plodding homeward with Willie Tucker holding a small figure, and she knew the venture had been successful. Her father and brother had peeled out of the yard early in the day, shouting the news that Simon had been snatched from his mother, and they were going to help. Sam looked as black as a thundercloud, and Collum, usually mild, was brandishing, of all things, the steel cutting-nippers he had been using to trim the gelding's hoofs.

Undoubtedly her menfolk would be home soon; hopefully they had taken the opportunity to pick up the mail and lay in a few supplies while they were in Meridian. Their arrival, and their account of what happened, would be enough excitement to cover her absence for a while. But she would be needed when it came time to get supper, so she hurried across the fragrant, fresh-cut meadow with its haystack, slipped through the fence, and turned toward the birch grove.

Her heart beat more heavily than the movement of her young body demanded; she was facing both an ending and a beginning. To contemplate the ending was for despair to set in; holding to the beginning—a new start in the good things God had in store—resulted in a sureness that brought a measure of peace to her heart and lent courage to her faltering limbs.

She saw, dimly, that the dead leaves rustling underfoot were like the dreams she had so recently cherished, once bursting with new life, now faded. But spring would come again; it always had and it always would as long as time endured, and with it new hope. There was a season for everything: "A time to be born, and a time to die . . . a time to kill, and a time to heal; a time to break down, and a time to build up; a time to weep, and a time to laugh; a time to mourn, and a time to dance . . . a time to embrace, and a time to refrain from embracing; a time to get, and a time to lose; a time to keep, and a time to cast away . . . a time to love . . ."

As a farm girl, she knew the principle of "a time to plant, and a time to pluck up that which is planted." For a while, in the spring, love had flowered, and it had brought a fragrance not known before. Now, though it was painful, the seasonal blossom was to be discarded, "plucked up." But in God's good time there would be another, better planting.

The sure knowledge of it was enough to carry Carolyn through the next hour, the lonely winter, and into spring's promise.

But when she stepped into the graceful circle of birches and saw Micah waiting for her, leaning back, his shoulders against a tree, his face turned in her direction, her heart faltered. But her steps did not.

Had some premonition preceded her? The man did not come to meet her. But he straightened and watched her face with an intensity she could almost feel.

"Hello, Micah."

Did her tone betray her? The black eyes narrowed. And his arms did not reach for her. A proud man, Carolyn thought, and I can't—I won't—destroy that.

"Micah—" She took a deep breath, dismayed to find it necessary to control a quaver in her voice.

A shadow darkened—if that were possible—the dark eyes. The mouth, so beautifully sculptured, tightened almost imperceptibly. Seeing it, Carolyn's eyes threatened to fill with tears. It wasn't going to be easy. Or was it?

Micah took Carolyn's two hands and drew her toward him. He looked down at her upturned face—on which the betraying tears sparkled—for a long moment.

"It isn't all right, is it?"

The tears puddled and ran. Micah pulled her close for a moment and let her cry.

Finally, stepping back and taking the handkerchief he handed to her, Carolyn mopped her eyes, struggled, and said, "No, Micah, I can't make it right, no matter how I try or how I look at it."

The man was silent for a moment. Then, as though half ashamed and half angry, he said in a low voice, "It wasn't a real marriage, you know. I had hoped—"

"You must have made her some promises, Micah. According to her ways and the ways of her people, she became your—wife."

"And I was a mere boy." The fine nostrils were pinched, and the line of his jaw tightened. "I didn't know what love was. Now I know. I know, and it's too late."

"It's not too late for happiness, Micah," Carolyn said gently. "But you'll only find it in doing what you should do. Go back to Chee; it's where you belong. And you have your daughter. She deserves a mother and a father."

Micah's bleak gaze was fixed over Carolyn's head, but his mouth had softened at mention of his child.

"Take her and go back to your—wife," Carolyn urged gently. "Or bring them both here and raise your child in Wildrose. She would be happy here, Micah. You could be happy—"

Carolyn backed away.

Turning away, stumbling in her tears, she was stopped by the low voice. "I never meant to deceive you. I loved you—your pluckiness, your sweetness, your weakness, and your strength—before I knew what was happening."

That same weakness turned her knees to water; that strength stiffened her backbone and straightened her shoulders and firmed her voice.

"Good-bye, Micah."

26

When the stubble gleamed in the fields and the frost nipped the vines in the garden, Jamie Jameson took what skimpy records he had and went to the Rooney place to give an accounting.

The three children were outside, taking advantage of one of the last good days, and the small room was quiet as Abbie bent her head with Jamie's over the various bills and receipts on the oak table.

Jamie's big hand clutched the stub of a pencil as he studied the material before him. Abbie, hearing his breathing, feeling the vibrant life in him—and listening to her own heart—found her world shifting.

Perhaps it was that hand—work-worn, calloused, strong. That hand, she thought now with a strange surge of emotion, had worked for her and the children; that hand had offered kindness. Suddenly it seemed typical of the steady, earnest, God-fearing man he was.

Jamie worked on. Abbie's eyes were drawn to a wound on his hand, a small gouge, one of many he undoubtedly suffered during the routine of his work. That fist seemed terribly vulnerable to Abbie at that moment. Her eyes filled with surprising tears; she blinked furiously and lowered her head over the table, wondering at herself.

With a final scribble, Jamie leaned back. "That's it, Abbie," he said, indicating a figure. "Not too bad, I guess. Do you have any questions?"

"How did you hurt yourself?"

Jamie's eyes followed hers. "That? Who knows? I'm talking about the harvest."

Abbie blinked. "The harvest. Why, everything seems fine."

"Sure?"

"Sure."

"Well, then . . ." Jamie shuffled the papers. "I suppose we should talk about next year. The crop, I mean."

Abbie looked at him with surprise. "I had thought we could go on as we were."

Jamie hesitated.

Abbie felt an instant panic. In that moment it was crystal clear, at last: her bravery, so-called, was bravado.

The truth burst upon her. Her performance had been a posture, a part well played, a defense against a world that was inclined to pity a woman alone. To escape it—no matter how kindly offered—she had smiled when tears would more accurately have indicated her feelings. She had sounded a positive note when she was really terribly insecure. She had tackled problems that had clearly overwhelmed her. And the assurance with which she carried it off had been pure pretense.

Abbie had turned out to be a consummate actress. Now, faced with the possibility that Jamie might forsake her, she realized how very much she depended on him, how he had been a buffer against the very worst fear of all, that of failing utterly.

She knew she had made a go of it—because Jamie was there. The fearsome darkness of her particular path had only begun to recede when Jamie walked it with her. And she saw now, almost to her horror, that in her ignorance she had brought him to the edge of making a fool of himself. And all so that she could perform the farce, the sham, of her proud self-sufficiency.

Jamie had always been there for her. Abbie's proud flag of independence had fluttered in the safe haven of his care and concern. Looking at that hardworking, gentle hand, Abbie saw it all.

"Jamie," she said unsteadily, "I've never thanked you for all you've done. I don't know how I'd have made it—" Her voice faltered.

"Nonsense," he said brusquely, folding the papers.

"Jamie—I mean it," she said earnestly.

"You would have done just fine," Jamie continued briskly. "There's no question about it."

With a sinking heart, Abbie saw just how well she had played her role. "That's not true, you know," she protested in a small voice.

"Of course it's true. You've done a magnificent job."

"Not really—"

Jamie's black eyebrow quirked as he said, "It's not like you to eat humble pie, Abbie." And though his words were caustic, his tone was kind.

Abbie saw that Jamie was about to go. And he carried with him the opinion of her as a self-sufficient, proud, independent woman, never guessing she was only this against the background of his steadfastness, kindness, and dependability.

With a muffled sound, Abbie thrust herself from her chair and began to pace the small square of linoleum. Jamie paused, his eyes filled with some concern.

"Listen to me, Jamie. I'm not really what you think I am—brave, and all that. "I'm—I'm really quite a coward at heart."

"None of that now!" Jamie said sternly. "It's not like you."

"That's just it! It *is* like me. Partly like me, anyway!"

"Abbie, if this is your way of getting me to take on the farm for another year, it isn't necessary. I was going to suggest you find someone else—maybe young Collum Morris—but I won't leave you in the lurch. If you need me, I'll take it on again."

Abbie hid the quick tears that stung her eyes by turning to the window, drawing the curtain aside and staring out blindly.

"The truth is—I need you very much."

Jamie, understandably, looked wary.

Turning and catching sight of his suspicious face, Abbie groaned silently. Chickens—of her own hatching—had come home to roost. Clearly, Jamie was dubious—and with good reason. She had been high-handed with him too many times.

"Well," he said, sighing as he pushed back his chair and began gathering up his papers, "I'll do it. I'll take on the field work for another year. Is that what you want, Abbie?"

Strangely, it wasn't. "Jamie, wait! You're not listening to me! Why won't you believe that there are times I'm overwhelmed, times when I'm lonely?"

Jamie's face was dreadfully skeptical.

"Truly, Jamie," Abbie said, and if her tone was pleading, she didn't care, "I'm not the—the Amazon you think I am! And I'm truly tired of those pants!"

Now Jamie's lips quirked. It seemed he would never take her seriously.

Abbie threw caution to the winds. In her extremity she used the one thing she knew he would hear: "I'm afraid, Jamie!"

Jamie's smile faded. Slowly, he rose to his feet.

With her face buried in her hands, Abbie peeked hopefully, and with some desperation, at Jamie's suddenly intent expression.

"Do you mean," he said, "that the job has been a bigger one than you've let on—to me, to anyone?"

Abbie's sob came out more real than she had expected.

"I don't understand," Jamie said, perplexed, struggling with this new concept of the imperious Abbie he knew.

"I have been—I am—full of fears," Abbie confessed, honest at last. "Terrified of the bush—of being alone—of coping. So I pretended. It was that, or buckle under."

Jamie's reaction was so like him that Abbie, in her newfound awareness, could have wept.

"Then," he said slowly, "you are to be admired even more than I knew."

His eyes were tender; hers—though she couldn't know it—were entreating.

The scrap of linoleum between them seemed like a football field for size. The rhythmic ticktock of the old clock emphasized the silence—or was it, she wondered, the thud of her heart?

"Abbie," Jamie said finally, "I'm ashamed of myself. In all honesty, I've tried to discourage you. I seemed to have a need to reduce you to the size of my expectations for a woman." Jamie was groping for words. "And my expectations were too small—for you, anyway. Am I making any sense?"

"A little." Abbie's smile was tremulous. "I think you're saying you wanted me to fail, so you could be right. And I'm saying I kept refusing to fail, so I could be right. And we've both been pretty silly."

"Let's quit this foolishness, shall we?" Jamie's grin was his old one, "—and get on with life."

"Oh, yes—" Abbie seemed poised for his next move.

But Jamie hesitated.

And Abbie saw the wound—the painful humiliation he had suffered when he had so disastrously offered himself in marriage—and she took the first step.

Jamie rounded the table with a speed that sent the chair at his back flying. Hands outstretched to hers, he met her in the center of the room. His hungry arms enfolded her, and Abbie, with a great sigh, laid her cheek on his broad chest.

The rising wind, wailing at the corners of the house, seemed to have lost its threat of fear and loneliness; it seemed to sing of warm fires, happy families, and loving hearts.

In its last burst of energy for the day, the sun laid a shaft of light through the window and across the floor, almost to their feet.

"Look, Abbie—," Jamie said "the shining light."

And though her face was lifted to his and her blissful eyes were closed, "I see it," Abbie said.